# MRS DONALD

# MRS DONALD

## MARY KEENE

*with an Epilogue by her daughter
Alice Keene*

EDITED BY
ALICE THOMAS ELLIS

CHATTO & WINDUS

THE HOGARTH PRESS
LONDON

Published by
Chatto & Windus · The Hogarth Press
40 William IV St
London WC2N 4DF

British Library Cataloguing in Publication Data

Keene, Mary
    Mrs Donald.
    I. Title   II. Keene, Alice
    III. Ellis, Alice Thomas
    823'.914[F]   PR6061.E/

ISBN 0 7011 2749 X
ISBN 0 7011 2750 3 Pbk

The publisher would like to thank Faber & Faber Ltd for
permission to reproduce quotations from 'The Kingdom' in
*The Collected Poems of Louis MacNeice* and from 'East Coker'
in *Collected Poems 1909–1962* by T.S. Eliot.

*First published September 1983*
*Second impression December 1983*

Typeset by Inforum Ltd, Portsmouth
Printed in Great Britain by
Richard Clay (The Chaucer Press) Ltd
Bungay, Suffolk

# Chapter 1

The train from the seaside had a compartment filled with schoolchildren. Miss Benson, their teacher, urged them to sing 'Choruses, so that everyone will hear how we love the Saviour!' and the children, ready to make themselves heard, rang out, 'Are you washed in the blood?'

The train rushed on, the sun keeping pace. Under cover of the song Rose watched the red and green turn swiftly to black. Unexpected green fields were a sweet reprieve. 'Not there yet – not there yet,' she called back to every flying patch of green. 'This will do – this will do!' she bargained despairingly as even the fields became dismal; overcast by the blackness. Finally she looked at black brick, booming home, her knowledge of it coming like her own shame to meet her. She was back where she belonged. The streets at home were her life gliding past her semi-conscious stare. She turned to the others with pretended excitement: 'We're nearly there,' and the excitement of homecoming, which had been gathering in little storms, came to a head, and the children, shrieking and clutching each other, rushed to the window as if to see all before them. Pushing her way through them she climbed to reach her luggage from the rack, reaching also for Ivy's, who had followed and stood waiting. As she put Ivy's treasured box of presents for home into her hand their eyes met with all the candour of the sudden glance. Rose was not thinking now, as Ivy was, of the comic handkerchief missing from the box. Turning away, she felt like a murderer, haunted not by the life he has cut off, but by his sensations at the scene of the crime, and the dreadful furtiveness of the dash on tiptoe to Ivy's cubicle, head twisted to look behind her, possessed her again, obliterating further recollections.

Holding the brown paper parcel of her luggage she stood behind the cluster of children pressed to the window, waiting, half oblivious of their happy murmur, for the gently sliding train to stop, when they would tumble out impatiently, calling to each other. Their voices filled her with the sadness she had felt when, the box opened, she saw the presents, and stood looking at them tenderly. She had taken the large comic handkerchief from her friend's locker, knowing she would be suspected, yet knowing she would never be accused – half feeling, as she saw its careful wrapping, the sorrow that its loss would cause.

They arrived at the Church Hall, then departed in twos and threes, turning to shout another farewell, or arrangements for meeting again. Rose imagined them meeting the next day, and for the rest of the summer holidays – lazing in the hot dusty streets, sitting in doorways bouncing a ball between long legs or crouched in a breathless intimate circle to speculate upon the trousers of the Reverend Mr Matthews with the creased groin at their eye-level as he preached before them on Wednesdays. Their exquisite freedom brought a sadness too crushing for her even to wish that she too might be there; a sadness she was used to, and had learnt, in terror, to resist. The terror of being lost to herself – forever split to the atoms from which she had come.

She unconsciously slackened her pace, holding back Ivy and Mavis who were walking with her, and they said with impatient grimaces, 'Come on or we'll never get there!' and she looked up, vaguely aware that she had begged them to come with her, and that they were on the canal bridge which

2

was always a source of comfort because it was a landmark indicating a safe distance from home. Soaring above was the enormous disjointed image of an advertisement. She saw quickly that Ivy and Mavis ignored it, were not horribly bewildered by it. She longed to ask what it meant but felt ashamed that she didn't know. Running swiftly, she leapt to reach the leaves of a tree, followed by Mavis, who turned to wait patronisingly for Ivy, who was too short to attempt the feat. Their eyes exchanged a soft subdued glance, the ghost of the glance on the train. Somehow overwhelming for these two, for though they were always together, and were considered friends, there was no affection or openness between them.

As they turned to walk abreast again, Rose knew that Ivy was feeling the blight upon her presents, with the handkerchief for her father missing. She herself had felt it, as she had paused with hand outstretched, feeling the sacrilege of even touching the tenderly arranged collection which had suddenly, intensely, reflected the constantly stifled unhappiness of her own life – but it had been easier just to take it and be gone with it in her hand. She began to talk jocosely of the missing handkerchief. But Ivy turned great sad eyes on the verge of tears upon her – always a sign that she was submissive, and the torture must stop.

Crossing a street, Rose felt spreading through her the consciousness that she was nearly home; overcome with a fearful excitement, she talked incessantly, arranging all that they would do, dazzling Ivy and Mavis who suggested they should walk home with her and wait for her to come out. The sudden terror (which she would rather die than show) that they would actually do this made her helplessly agree; wildly hoping that things might be different; the past a dream, the precipice she must rush towards, disappear. She talked on

3

now in a mad dream of home, incorporating all that she had seen and heard that day, of home's paradise. Had they not come to her corner just then she would have said they must come in, but seeing her home made her think better of it. Then her eye caught the sun as it shone in the short straight street; 'It has followed me all day,' she said to herself gravely. 'The sun loves me!' and – The sun loves me, the sun loves me – throbbed through her, everything dwindling before this great revelation, which would make everything different from now on. So blessed was she that she hardly remembered the aura that would surround everything. Then, seeing her home, she felt the shock of reality and braced herself to receive it meekly. With a quick catch of breath she parted from Ivy and Mavis, and rushed to the door which stood open on a gleaming, polished passage. There she turned for an instant, with triumph, to look back at them. She felt it foreboded such good, and walking straight through to her mother in the kitchen, past the beautiful portrait of all she wished her mother to be, she said with determination, but not daring to look at her, 'I have had a good holiday and now I must work!' The words gave her strength, moving her to tears, and longing for the stifling moment to be over she went to the scullery and rolled up her sleeves.

Standing by the sink she darted sly looks at Ivy and Mavis, longing for them to go, tremulously expecting her mother to shout, 'Aye, clear off, off the doorstep!' Mrs Donald did not shout, instead her lips twitched as she glimpsed in the child a terrible image of herself. But she was soothed to have help in the house again, and watched Rose now, happily it seemed, going about her work. They were calling from the doorway for Rose to come out, and she pretended not to hear. Mrs Donald remembered, as always when the child baffled her, a head injury Rose had sustained. Her face moved and changed continuously, her eyes darted around the room as if she'd entered another world where nothing was familiar. Then going towards her bedroom, with her eyes on the passage gleaming in the sun, she saw the children on the doorstep and went towards them gratefully, all her emotion dissolving into a great and poignant self-pity which could overflow any time in tears.

Rose stopped her work when her mother's back was turned, though now it wasn't to draw patterns with her finger in the wet. She didn't raise her head to watch her mother, but spread stiffened arms over the wet patch of stone as she waited for the dreaded words that would shame her. But they did not come. She looked up to find her mother talking in that different voice, chatting and smiling kindly in the way that made people think her an angel. Her mother was talking to them quietly in a wan voice, looking round the quiet street with rolling tragic eyes, interpolating an 'Aye! Aye!' into their conversation. Gradually they left, and not wanting to part with them Mrs Donald shouted another and another farewell, and that they must mind how they went. She looked appealingly at the closed doors of her neighbours, then turned unwillingly into her house, looking fearfully up at the walls as if there was something she was hoping or dreading to see.

Rose, who was exulting over her narrow escape – that miraculously Ivy and Mavis had seen nothing of her cringing at home, but had had, Oh wild joy, seen all that she had ever told them confirmed – her cup full, put greater energy behind the scrubbing brush, as if preoccupation with work, and the noise of it, would ward off every other contact.

Mrs Donald, who saw her, as she thought, going gladly about her work, admitted with comfort to ease her guilt that Rose was the best of them really. Her mind lurked uneasily

5

around the often baffling behaviour of the child. Her thoughts reached out to her beloved eldest son, allowing painful and usually stifled truths to appear, but helplessly knowing that it was there she must worship. She went towards Rose and together they dismantled the gas-stove. She noticed the child's tan, and thought she had had a breathing space from the misery of home; that perhaps they might start afresh, and even treat each other with the respect of strangers; no longer meeting only to clash. But, frightened of herself, she stood there terrified, helpless, eyes up for judgement, her last moment come. Rising as if against herself, like nemesis, she felt her great destructive will as she put aside anguished hope, and gave Rose the horrible great lumps of greasy iron to clean, over which she herself winced painfully. She told Rose she would leave everything to her when she died, eyes closing on that sole consolation of her life. But Rose hardly listened, or listened as one does to children who do not see the irony in what they say. As she took the heavy burden to the sink it seemed to weigh down and crush her hope. She felt the sudden weight of familiar misery, and, overpowered, sank into oblivion.

It was Friday, and the hard work of cleaning the house was finished. About to leave the kitchen, Mrs Donald hung back to survey the result with a grudging and savage eye, and as she looked round the overcrowded room every object echoed the words so often on her tongue – 'Your home's a credit to you Mrs Don!' – and defiant, she went to her bedroom.

In her underwear she tidied her hair, and her heavy arms ached. She turned her profile to the mirror, attempting to see the hair at the back of her neck, into which was twined a heavy false braid. Lowering her head she made this secure, then her hand reached down to feel her back which rose solidly either side of a central groove. She allowed her fingers

6

to reach further, becoming absorbed, comforted, bent double but unwilling to move, and wondered, her mind becoming blank, at the appearance she must make. Focusing, she saw the dark past telescoped in brilliant miniature. Great curving blades of flesh sank low and she might have recognised her mother in herself but consciousness left her.

She was roused by the sound of someone entering the house, and a look of fury sprang to her face as she thought of her clean step. Her eyes distended as she drew back the door, presenting herself in full regalia, dragon-like. Lennie was passing her with his bike, crude disgust on his face as he saw her thus aroused, and meeting his coolness her eyes sank majestically, threateningly back, in awe of this boy, the brilliant scholar.

With firm tread he took his bike to the yard. Seeing Rose he noted without interest that she was back; and she, her eyes vacantly attracted, followed his movements. In the kitchen he took off his jacket. Stretching his mouth as if the operation were painful he rolled up his sleeves, displaying a ruthless vigorousness which was part of all his movements, and in which lay the reason for much of his mother's awe. But Rose shrank now from watching him. Baffled by her emotion, she felt his belligerent unrestraint to be entirely lacking in beauty and grace. He gave off an overwhelming sense of the flesh, as does a carcass. Evening drew on and Mrs Donald sat at the huge table in the kitchen watching through the open doorway the brilliant patch of street at the end of the dark passage, waiting for the rest of her five children to return from work. As they crossed the threshold, becoming black silhouettes, she rose to fetch the meal prepared ready for them. Freddie went to give her his wages, anxious, for this one evening of the week, to please; then quickly, to show that he knew his place, he darted to the scullery while she shouted

7

instructions to Rose. Mrs Donald resumed her seat as they ate, watching, fascinated, the knives and forks handle the food, every morsel of which she knew, and the merits of which brought satisfaction or guilt to her face, which mirrored feeling like a child's. She raised her ankles to look at them wistfully if she was content, or turned away to watch her neighbour's families also returning home, her face straining greedily as if to catch what they said.

As unobtrusively as possible Violet was preparing to go out. She held her breath as she hurried past her mother who sat sentinel now, watching Billy who stood before her facing a mirror and also preparing to go out by flicking his hair with a comb. He was tall, and she turned her tired eyes to his feet which seemed not to grip the ground, but to lie numb in his twisted shoes. Laziness unchecked had gained a paralysing influence over him which she heard in the way he spoke.

'Tea, Ma?' he asked softly.

Rose was weaving her way through the crowded room, bent over a kettle she was carrying to the fire. Her mother's eyes bulged.

'Pour it for him, Rose!' said Mrs Donald in a pleading comforting voice. Breathlessly, surreptitiously, Rose snatched at those sweet tones and the use of her name, as if they did not belong to her. She buried them deep to ease the pain they brought, and forced from her mind the thought of his surfeit of tea, while she had had none.

'Ta,' said Billy as she pushed the cup towards him.

'Aye, aren't you going to say hello to your sister?' said Mrs Donald. The words were magic, and they looked at each other for the first time consciously as brother and sister, transported outside their dreary lives, as if they could take on new identities, as if a world outside they had thought beyond them was theirs to aspire to; a love they could claim. Rose turned from Billy's burning look to the door which had opened an inch.

'I'm going now,' said Violet through the slit.

'Aye, let's have a look at you!' cried her mother – gloating, malignant. Violet showed herself, guilty and timid, dressed in her best clothes, terribly pretty, her head an amazing mass of curls which she jerked back bravely, avoiding her mother's eye. But she was soon crushed by the withering look in which she saw her every hope of love, and all her prettiness turned on its nether side, and exposed as evil.

Rose hardened at Billy's pathetic look. His eyes had never left her and were fixed where they had wildly swerved to follow her moving head. She turned away, forgetting him. Dazed, she stared at the huge cluttered table which seemed an avalanche, impending to crush her hope. Raising her eyes to fading visions, 'Nothing is ever nice here,' she cried silently. She had wanted to say beautiful but the word was too much, and lifting dishes for cover she went to the scullery.

She was now behind the scullery door, spinning out the wiping of her hands for as long as possible. She now had nothing to do, and stood leaning to one side in front of the table, looking into the kitchen where she would dearly love to be; where Mrs Donald smoked a cigarette this Friday – the troubles of one week over and time to relax before another began, watching Billy heave himself into his coat, looking surreptitiously into the mirror as he did so as if to catch himself off-guard. Rose stood silently, afraid of being noticed, her body becoming slumped and exaggerating her round shoulders as she dropped into the numbed semi-conscious condition habitual with her and which caused her mother to remark, 'I swear she's not all there! Look at her, Billy!'

Rose met her mother's eye and turned away guiltily, shifting as if to pull herself together, confused, not knowing what to do; abandoned appeal in her eyes because she could not bear the injustice of always being sent to bed when the work was done. Mrs Donald saw her as a silent witness, full of innocent accusation, and was irritated by her miserable appearance which made her long to scream, 'Smile, can't you!'

Mrs Donald sarcastically softened. 'You can go out!' she cried with fierce eyes which looked ominously downward to see what she'd done, her guilty expression changing to hard satisfaction at being rid of Rose, exactly as when she said, 'Aye, upstairs!'

# Chapter 2

As Violet left the house to meet Louis, she gave a quick look at the baffling world of which he was the centre, and which presented itself to her mind as dark rolling clouds. She looked at them as they rode, images of mystery; burden they seemed of all her days – now bellying threateningly as she drew back, afraid of her ignorance. Straining for comprehension she soared upward; forcing herself into those clouds, recoiling, sick, from the vacuum. A world insubstantial – she cried out to herself, gasping – which made the physical world she knew unreal, the food she had eaten, the house she had just left belong to a bygone age.

Leaving the street she raised her eyes to the high calm sky, pink and effulgent with evening, her eyes fixing upon a glowing cloud edged with light in which she seemed to see Louis smile, his head held confidently there. She turned grasping at something, the brilliant cloud still fixed on her sight – the smile of the enlightened, she told herself – the great ones – poets. Louis was a poet and a painter and the awful fact made her see herself as a hollow sham, the belching clouds of sulphurous brown pressing down upon her brain, obliterating all she knew.

With her common understanding she must enter his great world, be blindly caught up in it. Oh farewell – she cried out to herself with an anguished thrust forward. She must get ready to act, and she felt tension grip her. Driving herself forward she looked down at the white silk blouse she wore, and felt the flowing breeze lift her hair, and raising her face she felt herself sail towards Louis – an unearthly creature like himself.

On the bus she imagined him – dark and magnetic, smiling indulgently at her old stupidity. On meeting him she had mocked him, saying, 'I thought all poets were pale and drawn,' and he had turned to her intimately with a look that foreboded this other world and which ever since had held her in thrall. Her head turned upward and she struggled from drowning in the memory.

Her mind remained quite blank until she saw the familiar streetlamp set in a triangle of converging alleys, and then on the shadowy pavement saw inevitably the pool of blood that she had been told had once been there after a famous fight. Overcoming a faint heart-sickness she told herself she must certainly be in the thick of things – in the midst of life; and the night quickened with a black glitter before her eyes.

Moving a few yards to the doorway of a café, shrinking from contact with figures muffled in dark as they passed to the basement below the scene of the bloody fight, who she felt must still be smeared with that blood, she put her hand to the café door with the revulsion she always felt as she did so; and she looked up to acknowledge that she shouldn't be here. But, lured by panic she opened the door to be greeted sweetly, as if in recompense, by sudden warmth.

Light striking violently from her white blouse made her close her eyes, and she raised her head. Sanctified by the brilliance which elevated her she felt above the grubby crowd, who sat as if engulfed in shadow. She felt everywhere that satisfaction in her arrival usual among habitués, and she bent over, greeting her opposite numbers, complementing their coming, and moving with the ineffable warmth of bringing her part of the evening with her. She turned to receive, broadside on, the heady impact of admiration from strangers who watched her openly, as if from afar. Their eyes became pivots as she moved before them in a circle of flame.

She chose, as usual, to sit next to Johnny, an old man rolling a cigarette who looked up as he saw her approaching with a forced expression as of the gravity of his years. He had never forgotten that she had once said she would come and live with him, and the memory flared in his dull eyes. From his side she surveyed the scene, looking eagerly to see who was missing, noticing Porter and Julian who regarded her jealously, openly hostile at a distance. But it was Porter's demonic eyes, lit above all with ideas from the books he was carrying, that pleased her and made her feel she was home.

Ann was coming to join them, raising cries of unctuous welcome, and Violet raised her head upon a tide of joy, bathing her radiant face in light, absorbing the comfort of knowing she transformed the place; knowing it beyond Ann's pronouncement of the fact which seemed to toll a bell completing an anthem within her. Johnny brought from his coat a photo of Violet, and showed it to her cautiously, as if she might snatch it away. It was a profile, severely lighted, which showed starkly the all but perfection of her features. Violet saw it didn't flatter her, and turned away, disowning it, but the severity gave her an exalted look and it was this aspect that Johnny treasured.

He pocketed it silently, touching a bruise in his mind. It was when he had told her he had this photo pinned to his wall that she had cried to him, 'Johnny! I myself will come and live with you!' Now he entered again the terrible maze where all seems possible and nothing certain. With her by his side he felt sharply that quality she had of making all things possible, of making his fears seem superimposed from outside – not his own; and, light looming, he saw her as a beacon of dreaded hope turning his water into wine. But it was that very quality in her that frightened him. He reached out quickly for himself in that great rosy flow and flailed out wildly for the anchors of his life. Ann, bringing coffee, was describing the luxury of Sunday at home, and they listened, cloyed by her pleasure. She had long, brilliantly white teeth which seemed to gnash lasciviously as she enunciated her words. She was Jewish and appeared to move in a medium of oil against the rasping dryness of Johnny's life.

'Come and see us next Sunday!' she urged Violet. 'Stay the weekend.' And Violet imagined them there, stifled among cushions, moving in the slow motion of comfort which made her long for air.

Johnny handed Violet a clock face, and slowly taking his time brought another from his pocket. He claimed to be the inventor of luminous paint, and raised an eye as if he knew he saw true pictures that would one day be painted in it. She handed back the clock face, resting her head on her hand to listen disconsolately as he spoke of colours. She imagined it added to the collection in his room in which he seemed to have no existence, and she remembered how their life to-gether had taken shape in his look when he turned to her with desperate light in his eyes looming from the depths of him, as if he were struggling back to life. She had plunged away from the dreadful nakedness of his need. It was too hard – it was too like the past.

Pocketing his specimens he began to grumble, and as he spoke of his alienated rights Violet breathed the sad suffo-cating sickness of this place – in which she acquiesced, as of necessity, with a far-off tender despair among the mad. She saw him, Crusoe-like, building with rudiments while shining all round was the brilliant edifice. She longed to turn him towards that brilliance, but shrank from what she would see

– his raised eyes white in that light, mole-blind with darkness.

He said he would have duck and green peas when his ship came in, and they both laughed comfortably – at home with all that this meal implied of sophistication, and Violet saw the future beckon.

Causing sudden disturbance like alarm among pecking birds, she rose to go, laughing inconsequently at Ann's dismay, threatening never to return, then relenting; seeming already too far gone to interpret Johnny's look which flickered up and held her hideously, saying she too would be defeated. She felt his age annul her youth and wrenched herself away, deliberately passing Porter as she made for the door, defying his hatred though she felt the violation of his look like a blow – the exulting hatred of the half-mad. Outside her eyes plunged to the ground. Meeting Louis was an altogether different business.

He sat in a softly lighted cocktail bar with a background of mirrors. When their eyes met she was struck by the immobility of his face and her own face immediately assumed a similar stillness. Nothing moved him. He must be very great, she thought.

Stepping towards him, she saw imposed on her eyeball, refusing to sink in, that someone was with him and felt an outsider, one of the crowd. Then she stood over him while he looked at her and she laughed, struggling for equilibrium, pretending to be unaware that she was making a forced entry.

He sat with Dinah who, raising her arms, asked what they would drink.

Louis turned to Violet, noticing the strained look on her face and the waif-like appearance of her hunched shoulders, grotesque in the smart bar, and though he relished the sharp contrast, he felt his weakness for smart women with whom he could relax. Violet became perplexed whenever aware of him – half aware – never crossing the border to reality, forcing herself from it as it met her like a brick wall. Louis was married. There was room for her only in dreams. It seemed to her that they stood eternally in the burning glass of the present moment – no past, no future; and her confused awareness of this was like clouds pressing down. She heard, as if in the distance, Dinah's talk of living undersea, and she watched her face in the gold light as she seemed to clothe herself, like Neptune, in that great element.

'I would rather fly like a bird!' said Louis, his eyes lighting as if in kinship. 'Birds have the best of it!' Yes, and he was a giant Condor, he told himself savagely; forever descending upon things like a supreme consciousness, and he felt the old pain bowing him as he succumbed again to terrible weakness. 'Casual pleasure is enough!' He revived himself desperately, guilt like vultures hanging over him. He held fast, gripping his antidote, and felt his great delight in created things slowly usurp him; things to which he would give himself entirely, not asking 'where or why the river runs' but watching for the shadows of swallow's wings.

Violet sat silently, obliterating herself. She almost no longer felt the agony of being with him except in the aching confusion of their talk. She knew by its very tempo – as if they talked of mathematics – that she couldn't understand it. When she heard familiar words they had a different meaning to the one she knew – added up to something else. Dimly she felt their words were only implications, clues to something hidden that was eternally being discussed. Louis was above her, free to think as he liked. He moved in a large world which made her look down and away in shame, as she saw herself, beneath him in her own eyes. With a full view of the bar she sat watching for the silent tableaux which she imagined were perpetually presented to him in the moving shapes and figures round them multiplied in the glass – desperately invoking the hidden deities to reveal to her what he saw. Dinah flung back her head in morbid ecstasy: 'To be self-created!' she wailed. 'But even the Gods were not that.'

Violet felt her like an undertow against life, a surfeit of sick dreams from which she must break away. She seemed always to have sat elegantly wailing there and Violet cut in on her drawl with biting words. 'Why don't you find something you can do, and do it!' she cried, her frustration breaking loose. 'Why don't you work instead of talking and moaning,' and in torment she fled from the place.

A moment too long but then Louis was beside her, looking up into her face. 'An undertow,' she cried, 'that's what she is,' and she glimpsed close the excitement that made his eye gleam. As if she was bound to excuse her tirade, and in defiance of the eyes that saw, and above all to be that person she must be for him, she increased her anger until she became incoherent. But she saw that he watched her dispassionately, enjoying her anger, not distressed for her sake. For a moment she refused to believe it, but his coldness entered into her and her own hollowness settled round it, and in grief she became quiet.

At the tube station they kissed.

'Are you coming back?' he whispered.

She saw her route homeward like arrows on a map urging her to follow. Home lay remote and still, curiously black and white, an ice-age from where she now stood. She hesitated and Louis was off. As the rattling train carried him away, creating between them a wider distance, she felt unbearably drawn out and unconsciously doubled-up. She turned blindly for the stairs, closing her eyes on foggy ghosts of people. All

17

life would be like that she told herself – ghostly! She was as good as dead until she saw him again.

# Chapter 3

'I thought you weren't coming out,' said Ivy suspiciously. Rose stood languidly in the soft glow of a streetlamp, embracing it with one arm, watching the loosely drawn-up knees of Mavis swing together and apart as she sat with Ivy in the doorway of a shop.

'Look,' said Ivy, nudging Mavis, and they watched a pregnant woman approach.

'She's ten months now, my mother said.'

'My mother knew a woman went twenty-one months.'

'It's three months.'

As each spoke the eyes of the other two fastened eagerly upon her, anxious for each to indulge her thoughts, hypnotised by the great mystery they could not fathom, a presence among them that made them one. An idiotic sensual expression grew upon Ivy's face, and avidly she challenged Rose. Their eyes met, wavered – partners in crime – to communicate with an openness which made Rose shrink. She broke away, saying, 'I looked up confinement in the dictionary and it said "brought to child-bed" and that's in the Bible,' she added, exalted.

Mavis and Ivy got up, Mavis rising incredibly high with everything about her thin. She looked at the pavement with a strained face, as if here were the black pool into which she had dipped her hand, arousing an always mysterious subterranean life – threatening as it heaved over, disturbing darting half-seen fishes.

They walked silently, slouching along, without choosing their way – as if this were a pilgrimage, or as if they were on the current of a river. The streets were narrow and twisting, interspersed with courts and alleys, black as catacombs; the blackness accentuated by feeble streetlamps which showed palpably the thick darkness. They had a preternatural sense for avoiding the river, completely built-in by wharves and warehouses, whose blind walls foreboded the grim and the real. They did not question from whence came the sound of tugs but said, 'Foghorns!' automatically when they heard them. They passed beneath a railway arch, all looking up at the moisture which oozed down one wall from above, fresh and glittering in the dark. They felt it to be sinister, yet familiar, like their own hidden sores and lice. Suddenly Mavis darted from them and they followed, finding themselves in a courtyard – warm and intimate after the dreary street. Light came from doors and windows where people leant. Strings of washing shut out the sky, and on the cobbles children played, half-naked, and so black that their yellow curls contrasted grotesquely on their heads.

Ivy and Rose looked for Mavis, recognising at once long bony children, all with the same wispy hair, smaller replicas of Mavis playing round an open door. Rose stared into the house, puzzling where Mavis could be. She stared, becoming slowly transfixed, at a table against which was wedged a huge bed, both covered, it seemed, with the same debris. She backed away by inches, and as she felt more safe came the thumps of terror. She had blundered upon a terrible lair and was afraid of waking some monster there.

She went over to Ivy, who was joking with some children, glad to have a laugh. She looked up, forcing aside despair on seeing the discoloured indistinguishable garments, and sank into her usual torpor, wondering vaguely what they were.

Gradually she saw Mavis carrying another smaller image of herself. She looked preoccupied and solitary as she struggled along and Rose felt she was somehow eavesdropping. She watched her put down the child, then went to her eagerly, crying, 'Mavis! Why don't you clean up the house?'

Mavis looked down at her, dimly bewildered, and they fell silent. She threw a puzzled look towards her home and Rose, glancing sidelong, became suddenly aware of the people who answered her look with expressionless eyes. Feeling she was being caught in a terrible net she hurried out of the court, calling the others to come, pouring out to Mavis how hard she worked at home, affording sweetly to indulge the truth; looking, in her fervour, as she realised with a shock, into unseeing eyes.

They agreed to part at the main road, and walked towards it, passing Mavis's mother who hurried, carrying a bundle against herself, and followed by a small child. She paid no attention to any of them. Rose, privileged to be thus accepted, felt Mavis to be real for the first time, and looked often up at her. Her head was bent, her thin wispy hair making a halo interlaced with thorns as she passed a lighted window, her face full of remote sorrow. Rose looked up at her with awe and reverence, becoming fascinated by the Adam's apple that accentuated so starkly the thinness of Mavis's long neck.

They were back at the shop from which they had started and Mavis left them. Ivy and Rose continued until they reached the main road. They said goodbye but Rose called Ivy back to ask, 'What's behind that wall in your street?'

'Only the railway,' Ivy answered.

'Is there any grass – you know – on the banks?'

'No, not much.'

'Still, you're lucky!'

They stood for a moment, Ivy becoming docile alone with Rose, who then sped across the road. Ivy shouted something but the heavy jolting traffic roared between them.

Hardly roused from the stupor which descended like a blessing, Rose went towards Mrs Timson, who lived opposite her home, and now stood on her doorstep holding something out to her with an agitated hand. This was strange, for ragged children such as she were ignored, or stared at as specimens. Rose shook her head instinctively at the money offered her, and with dull alarm looked towards her home as Mrs Timson did, then dashed towards the light that streamed, disordered from the open door.

In a moment she was out again, running towards the main road. Leaping, she felt supremely lucky, full of her escape. Freddie had 'had it!' not she; but her heart beat as she felt the terrors she had missed, making her run harder. Arriving at the fried-fish shop she pulled her wits together to remember every detail of her errand there. Then she hurried home, aware only of chaos, her footsteps driven by tension, as a wounded hand is shaken, shaken . . . Her usual wariness was gone as she hurled herself into the house, unconscious of everything save that she was in a vortex and it was spin – spin – everything whirled except the need to escape, the fierce calm which told her to be on the alert to get upstairs.

# Chapter 4

It was Saturday, a gay free day in the week of routine, and people breathed deeper, contented, as they woke.

The front door banged. Rose threw herself full-length upon the kitchen table, legs dangling. When the cat's away the mice will play, she thought, and the mad gaiety of the words made her throw up her legs in intense glee. It was hot, and she rested after the fever of her mother's departure.

Through the window beside her, Lennie, brawny in shorts, mended his bicycle. Though he passed to and fro, they were, from habit, unaware of each other. He came in to wash his hands, noticing Rose 'queening it' as he would have said, and he caught hold of a towel and stood looking down at her.

'It would be funny to see you caught like that,' he said, maliciously amused, as he thought of his mother; and because it would so be so fantastic if she were, they both laughed – their laughter increasing with screeches of glee at each glimpse of the inconceivable – their mother confronted by this scene which would be incredible in her eyes.

Still wiping his hands, he remained looking down at her, watching the rise and fall of her body, his face stiffening. He asked if she knew where there was a rag, but did not turn to where she nodded.

'I need it for my bike,' he said, and Rose was delighted to be told by this brother who noticed her only to tease her in a brutal way – why he needed the rag. She lay full of amusement, vaguely watching the flies above. She seemed suddenly enormous to him, her legs like pillars drawing his eyes to endless distance, so that he abandoned, breathless, the effort to look at her entire, and saw her cheeks and eyes, triumphant and secret with smiles as she felt his attention. He touched her armpit with his finger. 'You have grown your first hair there,' he said.

Rose rolled over at the touch. She looked through the window. On the black wall of the yard a cat stalked, and she went out after it. With some trouble she caught hold of it, and as it fought to escape she thumped it brutally until it sprang away. Then finding stones she stoned it, throwing further, forgetting the cat as she waited for the rattling stones to fall far away where she thought life must be different. She was arrested by a malignant voice which made her swing round, arms up, as if caught in a shower of arrows. 'I've watched you, I've watched you,' the ghastly cry rose, 'just wait until I see your mother!'

Behind the scullery door Rose caught hold of a towel, pressing it against her clenched teeth. With thumping heart and fixed terrified eyes she waited as if something further must happen. She was still there, rocking herself, when Freddie came in. He shook his fist, which appeared to be deformed, surreptitiously at his side. Seeing Rose he lifted it, concentrating on giving it a good shake. They turned away as their eyes met, both ashamed; both having in mind the trouble last night which she knew might easily have been her due. She felt guilty, and also triumphant as she remembered the glimpse of him in the half-dark scullery where she had looked towards the stifled moaning, to see his whole body crouching as it sheltered within itself. It might have been her, but it was his turn.

He turned on the tap, his hand becoming normal. Forgetting for a moment the degradation that had made him turn to the wall as he washed, he darted a look over his shoulder at Rose.

'Gone out?' he asked, jerking his head towards the empty kitchen. Rose nodded, shocked by his eyes which he usually kept hidden.

# Chapter 5

Mrs Donald was off to market, taking Violet with her to help carry the bags. As she went to the front door her eyes had become wistful and appealing, veiled in their softest blue, her mouth melodramatically long-suffering. Once outside her voice had become different.

'Aye-aye!' she cried musically, as if to continue a refined conversation. Pulling at her gloves she looked round at the neighbouring windows, where she imagined her neighbours watching behind the net. She sent a malignant glance, camouflaged by a smile, across the road and into the eyes of anyone who might be watching, and as she turned it spent itself upon Violet who stood timidly near. Then she took quick short steps, excited by the evening before her which she imagined as sensual with gratification, grunting 'Aye-aye,' deep and urgently to the vision in her mind.

Violet, who had been moved, as always, by the pretence of gentleness in her mother, stole covert looks at the impressive bosom beside her, looking away as she encountered the face, which now, raised in benediction, was so different, yet still had the hard look her children knew on the true face beneath. As they turned into the main road she couldn't help taking her mother's arm, fighting the emotion overwhelming her at even this pretence of affection between them.

Though she felt supported by her daughter's arm Mrs Donald ignored Violet almost entirely. Absorbed in all she saw, she spoke for her own satisfaction, only partly expressing her mind in broken sentences. Violet, dazed, did not listen or speak, or if she did she did so timidly, as if she had no right to participate; she was silenced by despising eyes, exposing her cowardice.

Arriving at the market Mrs Donald was so anxious to buy that she stopped at the first stall. There was nothing to compare with the pleasure and satisfaction shopping gave her. The privilege and power associated with her huge order made her feel synonymous with Mother Nature, decreeing plenty, and she talked of herself heroically because she was gay, calling the man in charge 'son'.

'This is one of them.' She nodded towards Violet, who was watching the oranges roll into the bag, and thinking of the idiocy of buying so much at this first stall, knowing they would walk the whole length of the market, she carrying the weight.

'Ten years I've been coming here,' cried Mrs Donald, moving away, and her voice rang out as if proclaiming a gospel. 'They all know Mrs Don.'

Moving with eager face into the crowded market, which was full of sensation, it seemed that satisfaction and benevolence were beaming from every part of her. She even confided in Violet as she caught hold of the hems of garments hanging for sale above her head. The market was colourful; gay and raucous as a music-hall, with all the violence and bonhomie of Saturday night. She loved being caught up in the slowly swaying crowd. Overflowing with happiness, she smiled encouragement and understanding to each stall-keeper.

'I knew your father,' she said to one, luxuriating in a truth which transcended mere fact to express her great fullness of heart. Seeing a policeman, she felt about herself, alarmed for a moment, making sure of her purse. Then she looked round

27

for Violet, shouting, 'Aye, the bags,' with bitter irritation as she saw the gaping Violet, who though she looked at every stall was tired and stupefied by the noise, and walked dully along.

'They're all right,' said Violet; her irritation calmed, her mother, though with a great moaning shout and wild angry eyes, turned to the stall-keeper who had been watching.

'Kids!' she exploded, infuriated by the word. 'Why do we have them? Why don't we all swing for them?' and tears came as she spoke of herself in a great overture to strangers. They fell down her face with a babel of words so unexpected, and yet so natural, that they excited fascination rather than sympathy, and the tragic tale which broke from her with blessed relief – overwhelmingly told in expressionless words – was a deafening bell she tolled, of which they could only hear the echo.

'Left a widow with five children – one born before he was cold in his grave – it's then you know what the world is.' Her voice rose. 'It's then you can talk. There are not many would have done as I have done – as Mr Matthews said when he was in the other day – your home's a credit to you Mrs Don!' The last words crashed defiantly, and her eyes, molten with tears, leapt formidably. Tears splashed on her hand as she wiped her eyes, but their expression had changed.

'But what about this Heath?' she asked with foreboding – all eyes askance at the infamous name – Murderer – and still at large.

When Violet, who had turned away at the first sign of her mother's tears, realised they were walking further and further into the market she looked, with melancholy, around her. The stalls, now shabby and badly lit, appeared only occasionally, and in the distance was darkness to which Mrs Donald seemed drawn irresistibly as if to the bitter end. As

28

they passed the brightness of the last shop Vi could see no reason for proceeding, and found it unbearable to go on. She scrutinised the pavements imploringly as if the reason why she must cross and recross them might lie in the very stones. She fixed her eyes on a distant spot again and again – a generous limit to help her endure. Repassing the lighted shops, too stiff to raise her head – I knew it, I knew it, she thought, and the fact that she had foreseen it made it seem like a dream in which she walked dumb and helplessly. Watching her prophesied steps she felt they were a part of truth still coming true; that she was making it happen. She saw herself step into a little boat – someone was cutting them loose from the slimy lock and they were moving downstream. She saw again the brilliantly lit butchers' – the same strings of sausages and a memory of weariness dragged her down. Plodding along, watching her feet cover the ground, blindly aware of light and bustle, she gradually felt helpless, then felt she was nothing. She wondered how it was possible she was moving down the street. She gripped the shopping bags with a twinge of pain and felt she was strung by her muscles to the two bags, and it must be they which made her move. Falling back into the numbed position, quite slack, she told herself gratefully that she felt no pain, and with the long journey home in mind this was lucky. Soon she was installed with the four bulging bags in the deep mirrored recess which was the entry of Rose's.

The pub was sumptuous with mahogany and glass and Mrs Donald entered imposingly, breaking into helpless smiles which she bestowed about her, naively gracious in this atmosphere which was rich with well-being. Moving with sympathy among her fellow creatures as if she knew them all, she settled herself naturally among them. She talked using the whole of her body to express herself with a great vitality –

a bursting health that was fascinating, dazing.

'I opened my door and there he was!' she cried incredulously and her great eyes leapt, galvanising all present as they spoke of the murderer. 'As God's my judge!' she gravely threatened them.

'Aye!' she screamed at someone who still doubted. 'It's a wonder I'm still here!' Her voice rose, vibrating swooningly in the air as it died, and she sat for a moment transfixed with passion. Then a flicker of terror passed over her eyes, and they leapt again as she looked down on the dreadful import of her words. Masterfully and still threatening, she grasped the newspaper on her lap which gave a photograph of the murderer.

'That's him, that's his hat, at my door for rooms he was,' she said, turning to them, and they could tell she was giving a commentary on something she saw. They were fascinated by her eyes which followed her words as though they were pictures.

'Every inch the gentleman, mind,' she warned, suddenly fierce, 'but you can trust no one these days and I could see there was something shifty about him,' and her confidence in her own knowledge of evil showed in a terrible look which was reflected on some faces near. 'He couldn't keep still – he had something wrong with his collar and he was at it all the time – feeling the rope.' She turned to them darkly. 'And he kept looking behind him,' she said, enacting this; and as her eyes rolled in witness they were enthralled. 'You look worried, son, I said to him,' and, astonished, they saw her face wore tender sympathy. 'Just out of the army, Mrs, he said to me,' and as her eyes rolled over them, haunted by the glimpse of him, she saw in every other eye a gallows glowing.

'Why didn't you call the police?' came a mocking cry.

'Aye!' she cried with a look of terrible venom, her arm

shooting out, overcome, as she was about to speak in flagrant disregard of the facts. 'Never you mind,' she commanded superbly. 'We know all about your lot,' she added with disgust when she saw her interlocutor was a youth. 'We didn't come all this way to talk to the likes of you. I've got seven sons of my own, and its a pity you're not where they are, at home studying instead of in public houses insulting widowed women.' But it could be seen she visualised the matter afresh, prompted by his question.

Soon she was laughing, rolling her eyes in gay flirtation. She relaxed so completely when she laughed that they were disarmed by a sudden intimate glimpse of her as though she were a child. Laughing, her eyes were wickedly gay but their points of light still riveted the onlookers, and seemed only the reflection from deep wells of life in her, and when they caught her look they felt she knew all. When she left they felt their energy had gone. They felt they had watched a pillar of revolving mirrors, giving a thousand gyrating images of themselves, and in their exhaustion were still blinded by the glitter.

Outside she pulled open her shopping bags for her acquaintance to see, delving deep to bring their contents to light.

'This is the sort of table I keep,' she said, proudly defiant. 'None of your dribs and drabs for me. Ten years I've been coming here. They all know Mrs Don!'

# Chapter 6

'Crisp Street?' Freddie enquired after his mother.

'Yes,' answered Rose.

He was still turned inward to the wall, washing his hands as if to hide what he did, loathsome with shame and misery which seemed to radiate from his hunched back. Intensely aware of him, though pretending the reverse, Rose waited for him to defend himself nervously.

'What happened last night?' she said at last, despising him.

'Drunk!' he choked. He knew she had no sympathy for him, but overcome with self-pity he was longing to complain. His voice was weak with emotion.

'I'm clearing out!' Though he meant them earnestly, he knew his words had no conviction, because he always said them on these occasions, but Rose felt a throb in her heart as she heard them. 'You wait and see – soon as I get a rise!' and Rose, in dread of him leaving and everything falling on her head, said desperately, 'I'll be the next!'

'Then Lennie, then Violet!' said Freddie with excitement, watching it happen. 'Then she'll be left alone!' These words gave them such a sense of doom and justice that they were appalled.

'Billy'll never go!' said Rose, and pitiably Freddie looked at the fact, confused by this great wrong.

'But he'll have to get married!' he rallied. 'And anyhow – who'll do the work? And who'll wash his socks?' This last thought made them hilarious, and was simple proof that there would be a change. Closing their eyes they felt within them the huge burst of a new world.

'Get our own tea?' his eyes burned at her.

'Yes,' answered Rose.

They reached for sugar lumps and tinned milk. As Freddie cut the bread old rivalries rose between them as to how much each would get. Luxuriously they ate their tea, disturbed only by the diminishing loaf. It seemed cruelly unfair that for their one slice each the loaf must become shorn of two.

'What happened last night?' She was anxious to know.

'Got me out of bed to get fish and chips, and wouldn't wait until I put my boots on – made me go without, but I couldn't.'

Rose imagined his bare feet flashing and dancing with terror as he was beaten into the street.

'She said it was what her mother made her do,' he added dully. They were silent for some time, sinking into themselves, then he looked at her questioningly.

'Shall we start?' he asked, and they began to clear the table. Hiding from Rose in the cupboard, he put a spoonful of condensed milk into his mouth, but she saw him. He offered some to her but she refused, and took a sugar-lump instead. They began to work in the kitchen at several jobs they loved. Rose on her knees rubbed the lino with paraffin until its faded red and green shone rich and brilliant.

'Wouldn't it be lovely if it stayed like that. Look!' she said to him.

He had taken from the wall a huge brass ivy-leaf which didn't need cleaning, and was rubbing it with all his might, leaning back to appraise the effort he had put in. Too impatient to make preparations, they went about their work in a slovenly way, and more slowly as they became disheartened by the drearier jobs. The room was soon in appalling confusion. Freddie went to the cupboard for more milk, reaching down the sugar for Rose. He did this again and again, their fear of the consequences making them reckless; his movements lizard-like, as if each time expecting to be caught. Closing the cupboard for the last time his eyes flickered with fear. 'Come on!' he said, and they worked in earnest until the room was finished and they gazed at it, moved.

'She ought to be pleased with –' he said, both trying to forget that before she even noticed it it would be ruined by the chaos of her return.

'If only she didn't shout,' he said, despairing of even this least and smallest hope.

They sat either side of the fender in the kitchen. Freddie, with his elbows on his knees, held by the wrist his other hand which clenched and locked. He sat rigid as if about to leap up. Rose, gently swaying, played with her hair, letting it fall forward. They were silent.

The front door banged. Freddie's eyes darted towards the noise and he sprang up guiltily, anxious to be nonchalant. An uneasy look of hope and gladness spread over his face, and his eyes, touchingly uneasy, were ingratiating and shy as he waited expectantly for his mother.

Lennie came in, wheeling his bike, momentarily shutting out the light. He passed Rose, who still sat, and trod with firm precision as if his feet were made for this one step. Sitting at the table, he drew round him the things needed for the radio he had made; behaving as if Rose and Freddie were not there.

'Get me a bucket of water and I'll let you listen to America!' he said to Rose, who watched him. She fetched the water eagerly, but seeing the earphones on his head knew he

34

had never meant to let her use them. He propped his head on his palms, his fingers mechanised to sense the delicate screws.

The front door banged again. Rose made a dash for the scullery, pausing at the door to listen. Billy appeared, easing first one shoulder then the other into the room. He took off his coat, trying to catch himself off-guard in the mirror. Taking hold of its arms he lowered himself into a chair. Jerking his whole body backwards to raise his foot, he unlaced his shoe, turning to look at the table as he did so.

'Shall I make you a cup of cocoa?' Freddie asked him.

'Will you?' he replied softly.

'Cut you some bread?'

'Ta!' said Billy in blessed relief. Unlacing the other shoe, he looked vacantly at the mantelpiece above him, his lips hanging loose.

Rose was deciding quickly whether a cup of cocoa was worth the risk of staying up, and she flew upstairs. She undressed in the dark and slipped into bed. She lay listening to the tugs, and her thoughts said: fog. She went to the window, straining to see into the farthest darkness. Happy, she got into bed, visualising at enormous distance a ball of fog – so far away the fog could barely be seen – and looking down upon this picture of the immensity of the world where she would one day walk blissfully, at home in a land of plenty.

When Freddie heard the heavy, slow, authentic ceremony in the passage he felt surprised he could have mistaken anyone else's for his mother's arrival. Well, I'm making the cocoa, he thought quickly, and felt that, as if by amazing luck, he had been given an easy part in a terrible play.

'What are they all doing?' cried his mother ominously as Violet opened the kitchen door. Then she appeared, standing in the doorway as if in judgement upon them, then she came blinking into the light. Putting down her bags, she pulled off her gloves, pushing her escaping hair back into her hat.

'Aye, we'll have that bucket away!' she commanded Lennie with a sweep of her arm. 'Breaking our necks will be the next thing!' Then she went to her bags, unpacking them. Parcels rolled on her palms as she pulled off wrappings, her tongue flickering over her lips. She looked with awe upon a magnificent haddock, giving it grave sidelong looks as she put it away.

'Aye, do you see the way they serve your mother!' she said to Violet, who was passing. She brought the haddock once more into view. 'That's the way to be respected – we want no other!'

She foraged in her bags. Turning oranges in her hand she filled her china swans with fruit. Every now and then came the huge crash of paper wrappings, which with a happy sense of bounty she crushed into great balls. She gave to each a bag of sweets and shaking one at Freddie she said, 'These are for Rose – take them up to her.'

'And shall I go too?' he asked nervously. 'Or stay up and wash up the cups?'

'You should have been upstairs before this,' she reminded him, swerving away, guiltily righteous as she thought of him supperless. 'I'm hungry. Are you Violet?' she asked. 'What do you fancy Billy? There're some pork sausages outside – get them, Violet, will you?' Violet appeared with the sausages, a plump raw pile across which a piece of empty skin lay as if dead.

'Who's been at these?' she screamed, beside herself. 'Aye, have you?' she blazed at Lennie, who was nearest.

'Of course I haven't,' he answered coolly, 'ask Freddie – he's been out there.'

Going quickly to the door, wild as she remembered his shifty look, she cried as if from the depths of a wound, 'Come back here!' – her arm pointing relentlessly to the spot before her. His very cringing inflamed her. With her lips gripped between her teeth and her face distorted as if by terrible pain she lunged at him. Grabbing his cheek she twisted him into the room.

'Go upstairs is it, go upstairs, aye, we know why you want to go upstairs. Hanging's too good for you. I'll poleaxe you, you dirty git.'

She hurled him from her, and then was after him as he dashed to the scullery. Grasping the first thing to hand, which was a knife, she grabbed him like a dog by the flesh of his neck, hammered with the haft deep into his head.

'It was her as well!' he screeched uncertainly, and in disgust she hurled him away; but, her fury unabated, she was after him again, pulling and clawing at his face and neck, which he covered desperately with his arms and hands. He moved them continuously about to avoid the blows. Except for stifled grunts as these landed he made no sound.

'You dirty git!' She began to move away. 'I'll poleaxe you – I'll hang for you – but hanging's too good for the likes of him! Drawn and quartered he should be and flung out into the bargain! Look at the trouble I had with him last night!' she shouted, her frenzy rising again. 'He's uncontrollable,' she yelled with tremendous emphasis.

'It's late, Ma!' said Billy, almost inaudibly. 'Freddie, get upstairs,' he called into the scullery, where Freddie crouched, not daring to move.

'Aye, and you're another one.' She turned on him with fresh energy, her hand braced ready to strike. 'We've heard about your bits of girls – bringing trouble to the doorstep, I'll lay!'

Billy pulled down his braces as he went to the door. 'You great slommock,' she was saying, 'look at him! Hasn't had a good wash for six weeks!'

When the door closed behind him she called Violet, and in the silence that followed she heard the tugs and remembered the neighbours. Distraught, she began talking to her cat with exaggerated affection so that her neighbours might hear. Watching the cat come forward, though hardly aware of him, his cold gaze brought a bitter sneer and then crumpling desolation to her face. She stood for a moment at the mercy of something, a broken victim, then she sank into a chair. Almost at once she felt pain in her feet, and realised she had been on them all day; she sat resting them, her hand upon the head of the cat.

She became gradually stunned by the silence, and afraid of disturbing it. Shutting her eyes she felt exposed and she opened them again. She had a moment of feeling the cat's head as a soft warm lamp in the room, and then as being as alien and malignant as the unknown which hovered near. She felt closed in upon herself, and her thoughts burrowed to where she knew guilt lay, justice and retribution. She felt in the steady ticking of the clock the presence of the powers-that-be, and knew that she must bow down. She saw into the dark past as if opening black pits. Her eyes darted over them, unable to see, and she felt glad she suffered.

Hearing cracks on the stairs, she cried out, 'Who's there?'

'Me,' answered Rose.

'Open this door!' Mrs Donald shouted, furious. Rose opened it, saying, 'I'm going outside.' She had lain, aching, until she could bear it no longer, and she fled to the lavatory. Opening the door something soft and black with hair on end flew out at her, and she was on the stairs again before she felt the shock. In bed, though she trembled, Rose knew she was safe, because she would never again venture into the dark.

When Mrs Donald thought of her bed every muscle went slack, and a burden fell from her. She suddenly cared about nothing. On her side, blotting everything out as she drew her shoulders round her, she felt conscious of comfort, and slept at once.

# Chapter 7

Louis woke that morning to a delicious sense of timelessness. He raised a leg and replaced it with a sense that an era had passed. He felt himself newly created and left by some God to wake in a thousand years. He looked down as if to discover himself – the incarnate hero – sprawled on a mountainside, the earth gathered up like jewels into him; and as his mind's eye ran over the symmetry of his form – its order bespeaking the author of order – he was overcome by his humanity. His head jarred backward, shrinking as if it would bless – O God, breathe not upon my neck – O Didymus, to live like you! He strained to survive his waking dread, the coloured vista of all his days moving on him in an avalanche – down which I cannot run the gauntlet, he cried, seeing himself bowed and naked, doing this. O greatest cruelty. He could turn from his pleasures, put them behind him – but to retrovert and deny them! He cowered into his pillow, succumbing to weakness and sleep.

He awoke again later, uneasily awaiting memory, holding back consciousness, unwilling to be disturbed, resting himself consciously to enjoy a free existence on which depended something he might be deprived of. Unconcerned, he watched his familiars glide before him as if he were slipping downstream; an onlooker who would slip away, and as if he held an ace in his brain, his eye gleamed.

Aware of silence, of gold light, he knew it was Sunday, quiet as an afternoon. Day of rest, of closing the eyes against

40

responsibility, letting things slide. Lying here as if in burning sun, burning consciousness out of the brain – ecstasy of non-existence! But, cruelly, Dinah loomed before him and he felt her like a steam-roller going over him.

He opened his eyes, and saw the sun dance in coins on the ceiling. He felt bodily raised to affinity with his muse – all else like missiles coming against him. O spangling sun, O dancing discs of light. This promise was the affirmation for which he must live. He asked no more than to love what he could see – the perfect beauty of created things. All else was blindness, ruin.

He saw his house and family, where all seemed arrested, as if expecting him. The image jarred him fully awake. He saw himself take a step to his chair, his footprint a permanent mould in the floor which now gripped him, and as he swooned in agony he saw Di's face harden to her look of age to come. His family's inalienable right made him feel he was *there*, his life elsewhere a ghost life, his arms held out in eternal dispossession. He felt Di's thoughts like rays exclusively on him, all her words assuming he was hers. He felt himself held in the grip of her mind, and knew, unforgettably, he must get away. Let sorrows obliterate me, I shall go, he affirmed, and he felt burst from him a sheet of flame. With excitement so deep he feared to consider it, he knew he must go – go back to France. He felt the ocean between them – the water absolving him in a sea-change so great he felt himself become another man. He saw himself in a vision of England – grey and Protestant, the water-colour mist receding from him, as he headed for vibrant sun. But most of all he saw that only thus could he escape to where home-thoughts would come from such a dream-like distance that it would eclipse the mind, which would be lulled in peace, perfect peace, with loved ones far away.

He saw the exuberance of the South, the consciousness of the people which revealed him as a slave, the vegetal growth with its visible will. He snarled, seizing his prey. He would create works with the same compulsion. He felt the agony of equivalent energy within him, and strained to take hold of the intoxication, direct its strength to his veins so that, giant-like, he could get it down in work that would stream from him in canvas after canvas, allowing him to stand upright for the first time.

From consummate necessity untainted by desire, he returned to make terms with the world, and knew at once he must avoid decision. He felt the knowledge tear into him like a cleaver, leaving him perpetually divided – his own self disappearing like a wraith in the midst. He became, then, involved in a welter of agony, reaching back into the past and overwhelming him with the sheer weight of all he had sloughed off, and learnt to avoid. He wasn't capable of a showdown with Di. He felt it was blindness, a terrible violence to act, to become a combatant. He must wait, as it were, for a magical happening, which he could bring about by awareness. He felt himself capable of the most exact alchemy, as if he held life like a bird in his hands. He knew he must become passive in the situation, allow it to withdraw from him into a state of flux in which a larger fate would intervene, and bring him, brimming, to the surface. He could exist only in that delicate state between positions – withdrawing from what would fix him, so that he might reach out and touch all. He refused to do more than glimpse a blind trust – that in him all might meet and form a new centre. He would tell her simply that he must work. His one unanswerable stroke. I must follow the light in the back of my mind. (Oh, how his frustration was concentrated in this.) That was what he would urge upon her if he had the courage. He must work in France, and Di had the boys. He added them instantly to forestall her proximity. Di is a fighter. He rallied himself guiltily – the whole family are born fighters. He felt his utter degradation in the refusal of his mind to form the words it urged – let *her* bear the burden.

He would always visit them – Di and the children, and already he saw them in a different light. He saw that once the first difficulty was over it was marvellous how everything adjusted itself. The chaos of the present was moving towards calm. He felt healed by a great peace, in the wake of which was a self he had never known. He saw they might even be useful to his work, and arranged them, almost placing them in position with his hands. But it was what he didn't know that left the critical gap – the inconceivable lying in wait. He must live through it to find out, and when he forced it it seemed like blood raining on his head.

He had an agonised sense of Gods to placate, of moving between them so that he might remain neutral, and he knew that his very relationship with her was a sort of obeisance, a formal admittance that there was an order to which he must conform. There was no pleasure in seeing her, but he feared to be without restraint, saw himself belonging nowhere, and in sudden terror knew that everything could become nameless. He felt chaos at his back, waiting to move, and knew he must toe the line. He did not allow himself to admit what he knew was his great secret. He could only survive, work by questioning nothing – as if knowledge itself meant death.

In his intense fear he felt like a hunted animal whose only art is to anticipate, and forestall – his eye always a leap ahead. With an insight he knew he must never question he saw he must wait for her move, and then move imperceptibly out of reach. Relieved, he knew she would stay in the country, and blurred in his mind her thought for the boys.

The bleakness there, like a shroud over her youth, touched him. He had caught hold at last of that wonderful hair and forced back the brilliant confidence of her laugh.

He would always visit them, Di and the children, but, cowardly, he knew he would forget them completely. He turned, appalled at the thought of the nothingness he would leave behind. He had a fantastic suspicion it would show in his work, in the abhorred vacuum, and desperately he told himself he had never loved her. She had been, as it were, a progress to freedom, an escape from his father. He looked back to those amoeba days, grey and watery, never his own. A consciousness in which only his father loomed. He felt he had suddenly become blind, and must feel his way, and his overwhelming instinct was to return. Now he could love her, now he could return, reaffirming. He felt his blood throb with a new knowledge of love. He could go back to her now, and find his peace, but he felt her still like a steam-roller going over him. And his art, which he saw always as a small flame, would be extinguished.

Desperately he reared himself, numb from this thought. He must stand guard over his flame, shelter it with his hands. It will not stand purging, his soul passionately cried. He felt the past come crushing him, leaving him maimed but for this one hope, his birthright. He felt the burden of work like the valley of death, through which he should have passed long ago, equipped with youth. He had a haunting sense of time, as if the minutes must become years if he was to do anything. He was late, out of date, maimed with age, and others were wrenching the tools from his hands before he knew what he could do.

He knew he had no strength for these thoughts, which would culminate in such agony he feared he would have a stroke, and he turned them like gunfire on his father. Why hadn't he died when he was sixteen? He knew his work was answerable – would have answered. Why hadn't it come earlier – that cutting off, in which for the first time his energy was released. A gap closed and he became one.

He felt that so much had been taken from him that henceforth he must lie stretched like an invalid, be embalmed in rest, open every pore to fatness, draw strength to his starved brain. Be asleep to all, known of none save his muse, for whom he would wait like a saint in a trance.

Perhaps it was time he shook off submission and came into his own. He felt, with exquisite frustration, the tortured darkness in his work – like coiling smoke, beneath which sheets of flame were waiting to burst forth. With rebellion that moved his very foundations under him he turned to where his terror lay. The finger of order had been on him long enough! He would throw in his lot with that freer, vibrant state of flux that was so much part of his own nature he thrilled in unison with it. He would become one with that natural order which seemed fluctuating with endless possibilities. The apparent disorder all round him was waiting only to be grasped and fixed. He had observed it over and over again. There is order in disorder, he cried, sustaining himself at a perilous height.

He saw the superlative brilliance of his future work. The luminous glow of poems and paintings, molten and burning within him. He felt the breathless ease with which the paint would come, and remembered the agony of his past work – crude and archaic – piteous examples of his lack of facility. He knew he was succumbing to great weakness – had already lost something that would show in his work, and he had a desperate hope that these thoughts, lying here, might mean nothing. His passion would atone, he told himself urgently, haunted by the form it must meet head on, and strike. But he

45

needed just once to trust to inspiration; give full rein to his passion; find out what was there. 'I am not . . .!' he cried out in repudiation.

He was surprised to feel a new vigour respond, reaffirming the excitement he had felt in France. He saw in himself strange depths he had never probed, from which came words as though from a thrilling accomplice – I am becoming myself. He seemed to grasp the clue to a miraculous reality; his mind bursting with image after image, in which he felt himself consumed. Nevertheless he knew he could do this only in dreams.

Exhausted, he remembered he was to meet Violet that afternoon, and at the thought of her frustration broke from him with such intense relief that he slept again.

# Chapter 8

That Sunday morning Rose made toast, feeling the comfort it would bring. She added it to the tray of tea she had prepared, then rearranging the cast-off dress she wore to make herself look even more grotesque, she carried the tray to her mother in bed – and stay there, stay there said her mind.

Mrs Donald smoothed a place on the bed, her head dropping lower as she saw the delicate arrangement of the tray. She shot a guilty look at the girl as she turned to go out, and Rose, somehow knowing this, triumphed at the recognition.

Mrs Donald was glad it was another, quite different day, when she saw Rose and Freddie quietly, automatically clearing and tidying, their spirits submerged by the aura of Sunday; only half-awake and lulled with rest.

'Did you get your sweets, Rose?' she asked in the mournful, resigned voice that admitted all was well with her. Rose, about to explain that they had disappeared from under her pillow, said yes when she saw her mother wasn't listening. Mrs Donald was looking for her bag, which she constantly hid, often forgetting where. Suddenly with a reckless sweep of her arm and a huge smile which she herself enjoyed, surprised, she offered money to the first to find it. Responding at once to this gaiety in their mother, which they seemed to know as a sign – as if of life emergent from a nightmare of closed lids – the three children in the room leapt up. Rose on all fours beneath the sofa, threw herself upon it when she heard the bag was found.

47

'Look at milady!' said Violet who passed, half-dressed, hugging a dress beneath her chin for cover. But Rose was out of reach of common touch. Slowly, with great calm, she saw the truth like heaven opening. It was to lie here unafraid, and this was all she had ever believed in and was familiar with. She laid her arm along the sofa to take complete possession; lolling, she took her place as the darling of the house.

When Mrs Donald saw Rose she passed her quickly, frightened. Then, drawn back to her, seeing her lying there, her terrible innocence making even the air about her inviolable, she thought Rose, who she had never been sure of, had become an avenging angel, and opening the back door she sang, 'Holy-Holy-Holy.'

Drawn back into the room, she began to lay the cloth, half pretending to herself, as she looked at the child's head, that it was normal for Rose to lie there. Suddenly the dreadful feeling of uncanniness left her as she thought dispassionately, Her brain's gone, and for an instant, her own head dropping lower and lower, she felt the chaos of bangs and bangs and cuts and bleeding that the head which she now couldn't look at had endured – and she felt she had killed her. Then she took pride and pleasure in seeing the girl lie there, naturally unafraid; she felt it was a new beginning, but then her face shadowed.

'What's the time?' she said, looking at the clock. 'I must get the meat in.'

'Shall I get on with the potatoes?' asked Rose.

'Yes – if we've had enough of being the lady,' said Mrs Donald, who began to sing as if she waltzed, years ago, as a bride.

She beat the eggs into batter with deep satisfaction in doing right, then placed it beneath the immemorial joint, whose heat and slow cooking seemed to bring calm and slow movement to every Sunday. Billy appeared, his face blub-bered with sleep.

'What will you have, Billy,' she asked, 'an egg?'

'Anything else?' he whispered, sitting down.

'Aye, what do you mean, anything else?' she exploded. 'How many do you think have eggs every day? Coming down at this time and that young Lennie up and out at six this morning – worse where there is none, m'lad!' she cried, calmer.

'Aye, I'm watching you too,' she shouted, pointing deli-cately with the knife at Rose, who started guiltily back to work. Mrs Donald now felt her way clear, as if she were a ship, and could cruise with her sails stretched wide, and moving with her like a greater presence. Walking through the passage to her bedroom she looked through to the quiet street, subdued by the stillness of it. Towards three o' clock Mrs Donald went to the sofa with the Sunday papers, the violence in them seeming a great threat – like her intimate self for which she must answer.

'Here's that Heath,' she said, her eye terribly knowing. 'The image of him as he came to my door!'

'Must be a clever man,' said Billy, 'to be in two places at once!'

'Aye!' she replied, urgently scrutinising the photo, brought near and up-to-date with murder, to its sum-total in an act in which they met and knew each other.

Rose alone lurked in silence behind the scullery door, looking through the crack into the kitchen. The impression was gaining on her that she had been forgotten about, and was now left to witness something she would be accounted guilty for witnessing. She stirred as her mother stirred, sensing the woman's every movement, and with a deep breath moved to where she could be clearly seen.

Mrs Donald lay uncomfortably on her side, fretfully dozing, alert for the smallest sound. Rose crept into the room, her eyes on her mother, and caught hold of a newspaper. Her mother's eyes bulged. 'Aye, give it here,' she said, with a look all the harder as she saw the girl's crumpling face.

'I need it for school,' Rose whimpered.

'If you need it for school then let them supply it, not your widowed mother with enough to do to keep a home together,' and she began – though she didn't want to – to read it.

'I need it for school!' Rose lied to herself, choking, her face in the towel behind the scullery door. 'I need it for school!' and looking up she saw the carefree faces of other children, and she gave herself over to wallowing in self-pity.

Towards evening Mrs Donald went to the parlour. She sat at the piano and played the solemn, portentous music she loved. Rose felt the whole street must hear and feel this music to be a benediction; and this house, from which the music came like a storm, to be something other than they had thought it. Her heart swelled.

With solemn eyes uplifted Mrs Donald began to sing, feeling herself flowing into the songs of exile, blindness, and clocks that struck the hour of death. Songs which she felt embodied sacred truths which stirred within her inklings of great depths of suffering and mystery to which she herself felt true. Sometimes in the middle of a great swooning note her voice gave out, but utterly possessed by the song she continued it within herself, letting her voice transmit when it might.

Lennie appeared. Her face screwed up when she saw him to divine what he felt. He had cycled to the country for the day and she felt invigorated by his effort.

'How was Mr Matthews?' she asked. 'Did he ask after your mother?'

'Don't suppose he knows I've got a mother – he's only seen you once!'

'Aye! Once seen never forgotten!' she pronounced proverbially, satisfied that this was true.

# Chapter 9

Violet went to meet Louis that afternoon, steeling herself to confront directly the mood of their last meeting in which she had been submerged ever since. There would be no surprise, she told herself – meaning glory; grasping at shifting light which seemed like her own white flesh emerging from a dark pool. All was prearranged and she was but the completion; the idea had gone before, all was over bar the shouting. It was as if she must wake from a transforming dream, extinguish glory like a light in her mind, and accept the ordinary. She raised her eyes to submit to untruth. Louis wanting her had the terrible inevitability of the houses about her, and inevitably she must submit, there was no other step she could take. She would not think otherwise; she cried out to herself desperately, anguished by the impending struggle. She would have to deny her convictions about love, which in a sudden summation of all she knew she saw illumined as consciousness itself, upholding her like her very spine – blinding her to the simultaneous necessity to draw away from him to whom she longed to get near. He was her lifeline. She looked at the fact grimly. He had thrown her a streamer to which she must cling, soaring behind him with wings to her feet. Guiltily she knew she was selling herself. She saw herself turn on the wheel of the world, obliterating herself as the ground rose to crush her. She would bear no more, she would bury herself three parts in sand.

Louis's step was a little uncertain. This walk across the

park was a little too familiar. It seemed to him like Circe's island, or the haunt of the Sirens rent with cries of wraiths from the past. He saw the haunted eyes of those in whom he had lived – never staying once the fat had gone. In a crisis of guilt he saw himself returning to succour them and felt the lifeblood flow from his outstretched arms, and death over-whelming him. With great solemnity he remained unmoved, watching them pass, accepting his guilt and his cowardice. It was his life or theirs and he had long ago chosen himself.

'Do you think I am awful?' He turned to her trembling, terrified that she had seen his implacable need.

'No!' she said passionately as if he were a child, and then was confused by the idea of judging him.

'Half and half,' he said to ease her, laughing as she cursed the wind which sent her spinning round to gather her long strands of hair into her hand.

'You are dressed all in navy blue!' he teased. He looked into her eyes as if into a faery castle where he would enter and be immolated in delight. He felt he had attained, come into possession. His face stared irresistibly, and her heart went out to him.

They set off, light-hearted now, to cross the park, eagerly and irresponsibly as if to some unknown delight, innocent in a world of innocence. Louis thought of his wife left deliciously behind. He would walk with Violet now for days on end and she wouldn't disturb him. He felt himself leaving her in heart and mind, insulating himself in experiences she should never know, placating himself gluttonously with sweet revenge. And Violet too felt that they were leaving all behind, that they were walking in this wind as if in outer space without landmarks. She battled with her mind not to admit not knowing, but to feel only the oncoming gusts whirling her to white clouds. As they arrived at the flat Louis looked up, knowing he would not see those wraiths, but he knew they were there and if he listened he would hear their volleying cries, like Furies passing. He turned the key, naive delight in his success on his face as he let her in, and Violet, head lowered, felt she had been neatly trapped.

Aware of squalor, she did her best not to notice anything. Then to her horror – witnessing her shame – Dinah rose, grotesque from among the rudiments of home.

'You know Cedric too!' cried Violet, starting on a frenzy of talk to show that she was just like them, that nothing embarrassed her. She brought Dinah all her sympathy in talking of this homosexual as if he were quite normal. She closed her mind to the terrible prison, a vault overhead – her arms stretched in the dark to sense the atmosphere, the storms of disorder that rose from volcanoes at her feet.

'I modelled once at his art school – it was fantastic,' and as she talked of prodigious life she knew that they felt her mind like walls which she circled, unclasping memory after memory to show herself naked to them. Louis looked at Di to say they had arrived, were in mid-stream. He was hampered by the necessity to respond. This might go on, something might happen. He felt Violet flow over him like bright light, and himself flow back as if she was bringing him a wonderful new species of love. Excitement mounting in his chest, he moved round making tea – half in fear of his blank mind, like a dark sky, that must bridge the gap to her brilliant youth.

'But that's Cedric's great thing!' Di cried, emphasising the last word as though it were unnamed private ground which they must inhabit and make real. Violet felt clouds, like curtains, closing her mind; cutting her, agonised, off from Dinah, their eyes meeting in one last desperate leap over vast seas that might drown them.

Louis looked to Dinah to say his life had expanded –

flaunting Vi as a larger self. His eye was cool and accusing as if he had been robbed or kept prisoner in his wife's mind and now was leaping from it like a tiger. Violet saw them shocked into meeting and her eyes closed upon a conflagration into which all her faculties seemed to be falling. She saw the glow of a fire and fled towards it. Lifting a poker she poked it, all else was strange – she told herself, turning; she would notice nothing else.

As Louis watched her hugging the fire, he felt her dangerous connection with misfortune snake up over and adhere to him as though it were wreaking some terrible metamorphosis. He watched Di bringing the pot, their eyes meeting, as if in the future the ground would be cut away by an obsolete past. Di turned, her elegance accentuated by uncertainty, and surrounding her like a dimension. Her head dropped as she called them to tea. Their voices were like a tropic glow outside her wintry hollow from which the birds had long flown.

As Violet pulled out her chair to sit down, she felt caught in a hideous illusion like a ghost in a puppet world; chatting to them gaily while her real self lay struggling, limbs thrashing beneath her.

Louis ate gluttonously, scooping cream into his mouth, moved with love of it; and Dinah watched, gratified that she could comprehend him. Louis was wonderful when he was amused, when they could stand apart and be two people. She felt the importunity of the man's need like breath on her neck, satiating anger with a vision of some terrible maw from which flared venom, fork-tongued. Horrified, she saw it deep-distilled; ever-present but hidden. But Louis was wonderful, wonderful – she told herself quickly – the true person sanctified like a child in her mind, blinded by the light he held passive and innocent within himself, and hers to protect.

And she knew him, she knew him with an awareness of magnitudes in which all would be given through him who knew all.

Louis watched Violet. He wanted her to raise her eyes to his. Dinah was presiding, helping her to tea. She was too deliberate and too slow; cool and indomitable like reason – crushing him. It was as if he must shower her with attention, and then her eyes would be raised to his in happiness. He watched her look to the wall opposite. 'Delacroix,' he said, thinking she looked at the drawing there. She did not, but turned, relieved. Louis felt her timid trust as she looked at him from beneath her hair with a wonderful fiery glance like swords of valour – piercing him, inviting him to her side where she stood in glory ready to make possible every single dream. All else was unreal. He must step beside her, ride with her, close a door upon them. His eyes fastened on hers, rested upon her. He felt he must be absolutely committed to her until his dead weight rose, phoenix-like.

Di felt them near her, smiling like children, their shapes expectant – ready to interlock. She felt Violet come, purging the past and sweeping them on to a party mood before which reality faded, became unreal. But awareness came like a parting shot. Louis hung on to her in oblique submission, in fear of fears which neither would recognise but warded off with careful steps.

Then smiling, as if vowing themselves, they brought Violet their albums and Louis watched as if she were about to open like a rose. Veiling her face she saw their youth, ruthlessly smart, and hardly dared to look at the vulnerable faces which seemed to peer through with all the pathos of their secrets.

'Us at your age!' said Louis, smiling, looking at the snapshots through her eyes, a generation removed; like a child with a whole range of experience beyond him which he craved. He was so glad he was succeeding with her. It was as though she was a magnet gathering remnants of himself together.

'Our grand friends,' he laughed maliciously. 'We wouldn't be without them.'

'Not grander than you!' she gaily mocked him. 'The greatest man of his day!'

'You have found someone to tease you back at last!' said Di.

Louis looked to Dinah – showing Vi to her – remembering it was she who had found her for him. She was here, she was here, and she made such a difference.

'Is Dinah dark or fair?' he asked. They both looked at her in collusion, smiling, confident but their mouths expectant.

Violet hedged, arms up, circling instinctively for the clue to the words they waited for, for which they hovered, so that when she spoke – commenting only on details which they hurriedly filled in for her – it seemed as if she spoke from the inside of their brains.

'Darling,' they cried. 'Darling, darling.'

They sat back delighted with her, and intensely gay, as if, with raised arms, they had shuffled off mortality. She was their new idea, their new dimension, the new real-life heroine of a romance they were beginning, and everything she said was right.

Louis played with the cat, screwing paper into balls and driving the animal mad with the skittering sound; watching Violet as she lay on the floor, holding out bare arms so tender they seemed threatened. Her mind was reverberating with the terrible albums and she felt she had unconsciously passed some test. Louis longed to lie close, immolated in her heart, to know with perfect knowledge the dream of herself in which she was incarcerated – cut off from him and in which she held him cut off from himself. He could not believe his arms could surround her, encircle her. He knew she would stream like light through his arms as if he was encircling life itself –

Dinah watched, and felt him enter into her, deliciously sustained, his face gaping and quivering as he felt along her every nerve, his face grotesque as it seemed to take on hers, standing there simple as a child, raising his head as she showered over him. He had no other self but her and she felt the burden of it. Until he had absorbed all he could not be satisfied.

Dinah watched Violet talking unconcernedly about films, her face averted and half hidden by her long hair, as if she was holding another dialogue. Dinah filled herself as Louis was doing with the luxury of her beauty, daringly watching the intensity of her eyes in which her timeless spirit showed.

'You must come and see us all the time!' she said, knowing they would win the girl, and immediately she felt the relief of it and looked toward Louis – drawn by a need to attain with him the unattainable. She relaxed, relieved of a burden which seemed Atlas-like, glad to be outside the magic circle in which they were inextricable, and from which their sole exit was through each other. She sat, limbs wreathed against the cold, gazing into the unrealised past as if caught inside a crystal. She closed her eyes in unmentionable regions where necessity was revealed and passed in symbols through her hooded mind.

Louis saw her as a terrible constriction cutting him off from something vital, transfixed by deadlock in the past where she took refuge; her eyes turned upward to that awesome beauty let loose in consummate dreams. He felt himself a wraith in Dinah's mind where nothing crystallised except for mocking gargoyles who told him he would never know.

He took Violet quickly to another room. She saw that it

was dark and bare, deserted like the haunts of rats, with objects upon the floor which her mind refused to identify. In a corner was a bed of which she noticed only that it was hideously like those she knew. Once on the bed the need for pretence was over. She rolled herself toward the wall, shutting her mind to what might happen. It was something he wanted – not she, and she felt it hardly concerned her. Louis went over to her, the divested hero. If only he could keep her permanently subdued as she was now – as Di was subdued to him. He felt the desolation of his cowardice which made him finally a child. Women always knew. He longed to start something inside her so that she would accept him as a man. Through his child she would love him – Him! At the thought of himself he almost wept. He saw himself in this image as if tucked away, a blind spore inside her that must come to birth.

At last he took her to the balcony in the sun, spreading covers for her. He noticed that when she was naked her hands seem too large and felt glad that he had managed to see this. She hitched his black leather jacket onto her shoulder. It was terrible in the heat. Though she did not relax she felt she could afford to, and threw back her head in self-satisfied laughter. Louis felt it like boredom quickly destroying him, wiping his imagination clean of love. It was as if black desecrating hands had come up over her, and laughed their presence at him from her teeth.

Violet felt she belonged to Louis, that the past was over and the future had come. It needed only that she be the person he wished her to be, to act, or rather live the part he wished her to play, live up to the idea he had formed of her, be the pale suffering unearthly creature he had discovered – be a poet like himself, and figure in his dreams.

Emerging from the house, she still dressed in the leather

59

jacket – the burning heat of which balanced another agony inside her – they walked to the tube, she looking aghast at the familiar back streets as if such lewdness were new to her.

# Chapter 10

That Monday Mrs Donald turned, half awake, burying her-self deeper in bed as she tried to bury herself deeper in sleep. When the factory hooter sounded she opened her eyes, simul-taneously realising and pushing away the horror that she had held closed beneath cowed lids. She threw her white legs over the side of the bed; as she bent to feel for her slippers all her worries flooded over her, and forced her to a wild optimism to hold them off. When she stood she felt better, glad to be up, though as she moved her great weight she felt immeasurably old.

Later she stood over a bath of washing, her hair becoming loose, while Rose stood over a bowl of much dirtier things in the sink. Each time Mrs Donald carried her things out to dry she trilled a song, sometimes a hymn, that seemed to come automatically as she put her foot into the yard, though she was often breathless. Becoming suddenly aware of the time; of hours of work not yet, perhaps never to be done, she felt her work this morning had been in vain and that all work was useless. Overcome, she groaned and felt she must crumple on the spot. She caught sight of Rose who stood, deformed, entirely slack in despair because of the washing which she knew would never come clean and which she loathed touch-ing, holding onto the same piece which she had mechanically rubbed almost dry.

With a sudden movement, jerking Rose to life, Mrs Donald was yelling frenziedly, 'The water – the water – put it

61

in the water!' Then, her eyes closing, her head dropped backward as she gave out a great cry which came with infinite relief, 'Oh the pain – pain – pain of her –'

Rose flew into terrified motions of work, all her senses on guard for what might follow, trembling and flinching at her mother's every movement. Mrs Donald, recovering as Rose steadied herself, banged things about to emphasise her shouting. She saw the child's eye, swept down for cover, helplessly watching her, and in sudden loathing pushed her broom aside as if to strike, at which, in a convulsive jerk, Rose knocked her bowl over, drenching herself from the chest down. Rose now stood beyond terror, almost unconscious. She lifted her bloodless face as if she were about to die, and from her came the hiss of water. Looking down the mother saw incredulously the urine rushing down the child's legs. For a moment she stood aghast, looking with awe upon the face held up to her with unseeing eyes. Then she saw the pool on the floor and was overcome with familiar fury. With a terrible distortion of her face she clutched Rose by the hair, forcing her down, rubbing her face in the pool, shrieking of her filth, that she had dared do it. And as this last occurred to her she was maddened so that she feared for her reason. She lifted her head wildly with a scream, and felt such violence within her that, as she belaboured the child, she knew with terror she might kill her and saw vividly her bursting head. Dragging Rose to her feet she hurled her into the kitchen, screaming, 'Get out of my sight,' while the child stood clutching the table, her blurred face moving stiffly with the stifled moans that gave vent to her terror.

'Upstairs!' she shrieked with a rush at the child, her face moving with her arm in a terrible slow sweep; the terrible pincer of finger and thumb twisting, garrotting, and now driving upward as if through the child's sex.

62

As Mrs Donald turned back to her work, she heard within her the ghost of a voice – 'She's only a child!' She now found comfort in her work, looking upon the humbler jobs even as a blessing. With her mind fixed on Rose she felt rise within her a deep quiet and awe, as if Rose had sprung up like a magic shoot and she herself had fallen away.

Hearing the latch of her neighbour's door she ran to her to defend herself, calling with an outraged expression, 'Did you hear what I've been through with that dirty mare – in front of my very eyes!' Mrs Donald screamed incredulously. She talked hurriedly with a hopelessness that made her sigh and muddle her words. 'Nobody knows!' she cried at last, to make an end. Then with a malignant gleam of interest in her eye she said, 'Only the other day I came across her, twisting herself about in front of that young minister.' "I'm going to marry you when I grow up . . ." That was her,' and Mrs Donald gave a ghastly imitation of innocent childishness. 'There're no lengths she won't go to – you look out for your two boys!' she cried with hidden derision. 'I'm warning you!' As her neighbour talked Mrs Donald looked up at the window opposite which reflected that of Rose, and felt within her the quietness of before. Then with a cruel look away – I'll lower her, she thought. 'And yet when she wants to behave there's no one like her – which makes it ten times worse!' she cried, angry again.

Above her mother's head Rose, lying on her bed, opened her eyes and saw the next-door window through her own. She stared at the hard white patch of light where the glass was naked, which sooner or later would pose the inevitable question: What was there before there was anything, when there was nothing? She drew back as if from infinity. As if, turning pages with breathless impatience, she disposed (as she had done so often) of everything in the world. Her eyes widened as the window-pane began to spin, to fight the whirling emptiness which would catch her up in the unimaginable image that blotted all out. What was there before there was this?

She heard her mother on the stairs and held her breath. Mrs Donald never came into this room, but Rose didn't think of this and then she knew that her mother stood over her.

Mrs Donald thought Rose was deep asleep. And what are her dreams? she wondered. Rose opened fixed, unseeing eyes full of suspense – the enormous pupils crystallising with terror as consciousness came. 'Aye – get up and we'll look at this bed!' her mother said to bring her quickly to her senses. She pulled the mattress, folding it in two, at which a great army of disturbed bugs began to move like a spreading pool of blood.

With an arm that seemed to rise with awesome portent as if from the dead, Mrs Donald pointed to the stairs 'The paraffin!' she gasped.

# Chapter 11

With a blast of traffic which made her spring into the air Rose was swept into the delicious privacy and freedom of the main road. School tomorrow, she thought, and with a rush of joy seemed to fly there on wings. To hold herself back she forced the thought from her mind. She began to run, then stopped. I mustn't hurry, she thought, wincing, gasping at memories of enforced slowness on the way back. She walked slowly, rhythmically, watching for where the pavement dust was lifted to swirling eddies or dunes by the wind, pressing her feet deliberately into them and looking back for the impression. Finding none, she continued as gradually her spirit left her, and she became stupefied; her body so slack that in parts it appeared broken. The bottle filled, she turned homeward, making detours to stretch out the time until she saw, with pride, the good appearance of her home – straining to hold on to this waning vision as its heartbreak seized her. Then with a great swing of her head downward she rushed towards the house as if to a collision. Looking fearfully up at the door she saw close the grain of the wood, and felt a bewildered and terrified stranger here.

It was dark inside and Rose grabbed fruit from the heavily laden table.

Mrs Donald came urgently into the room, her arms moving at her sides, a small vegetable knife she had used long before still held in her hand.

'Hasn't he come yet?' she exclaimed, surprised, looking

65

towards the clock and lifting a chair. 'Here, son, sit here, there is more room for your books.' She spoke to the young student who waited for Lennie. 'I've just been over the road,' she said, pondering this and indicating the house opposite, 'and they'll be coming for me again, I'll lay, before I'm much older!' She threatened death with terrible eyes, then turned back to the street, watching the house opposite where Ben's wife lay dying. Hope rose in a sudden billow over her head and she gasped, flooded with warmth. 'You should see him over there,' she said wistfully. 'Poor lad, using the dish-cloth for everything!'

'How are you getting on, son?' she asked, comforted, not minding that he had not heard. 'Our Lennie's just won another exam!' she said, suddenly animated. 'He's a lovely boy! pity his father isn't here to see him! And he should never have died!' she cried, suddenly fierce. 'But what we live for I don't know – except to bring children into the world who do nothing but bring grey hairs to our heads!' This was directed at Rose, who cringed. 'And what I've been through with that one in there would bring down twenty heads, never mind about anything else! Where's the paraffin,' she cried, re-membering, 'and the change?' Rose put the money where she drummed on the table. 'Did you get it at Jackson's? Did he ask after your mother? Then take this and go!' She pointed with a piece of bread into the yard, 'And mind the washing with that filthy head!'

'What man will ever have her?' said Mrs Donald, relieved by the necessity of dispensing with Rose.

'She's good-looking really,' said the boy.

'Yes – she's got a nice skin,' said Mrs Donald thoughtfully. 'My mother had a beautiful skin, and their father was a lovely man.' She grew fierce. 'Otherwise he would be here to this very day.' She flinched as she spoke as if the dead came catching her up. 'One in a thousand he was, and wouldn't hurt a fly! He fetched them all down!' She shrank in her chair, arm raised to ward off the sight. 'Only babies they were, and laid them along that wall – she indicated with her knife – 'and drew the sign of the cross over them – and then I sent for his brother!' she added, relieved by the change of scene.

Grasping the apple trees, Rose climbed the wall at the bottom of the yard, becoming excited, half expecting to see a miracle or some great wonder of beauty in the garden. She looked into where all was laid out and arranged, avoiding with a pang the dark green of this old shrubbery, stretching her neck to see if the order extended, positively to the back door.

'Help me over and I'll help you!' she cried, eager and excited as she saw the old man struggling with roots, her excitement rising unbearably as she imagined her feet touching the ground beside him.

'What's happened to your face?' he asked.

'I fell!' answered Rose, dropping out of his sight.

'Aye, here he is!' said Mrs Donald with round eyes, rising as Lennie crossed the step with his bike. 'Your Indian friend has been waiting half an hour!'

'Not Indian, Ma!' said Lennie, frowning.

She halted to look up at him as he passed, moved by memory, saying as she searched him, 'Look at his square head!' as if she would fathom through him his father, and through him fathom her son. 'You are, aren't you son?' She smiled gaily to the boy. 'Anyhow, I've never seen such teeth. I'm sure your mother's proud of you, and you cherish your mother, son. We have only one mother in this world, and a boy's best friend is his mother. Aye! Tell her to come in!' she said, pointing with her knife as Lennie returned, and suddenly she came upon Rose.

'You're a specimen!' she said, exasperated. 'Aye, off with those clothes and under the tap. I'll look at those!' she cried malignantly, as Rose seemed about to hide her clothes. 'And I'm watching you, don't forget!' she cried in the midst of cutting bread. She noticed, moved, the shoulderblades set in the child's back as her own were. 'Aye! The armpits!' she screamed as Rose shrank from the cold water. 'Or I'll be in there to show you –!'

Lennie lifted his head to frown at the noise.

'Aye, – and you're another one, m'lad! We'll have an inspection of the whole lot of you – above and below,' she cried audaciously. 'You know what I mean!'

She brought Rose a spotted dress, preparing herself for what she would see.

'Aye, put this on!' she said sternly.

The dress left arms and neck bare. She looked at the girl to descry the good looks she had heard mentioned and which she felt might exist although she couldn't see them, but was overcome instead by the sight of soft clear lines so fresh and fragile it seemed they would disappear if she touched, or looked too long. Youth, she almost thought, but overcome by the word she could not.

# Chapter 12

It was early morning. The door banged behind Rose as she set off to school and the house was still. Mrs Donald paused unconsciously. I'll get down, she told herself fearfully, eyes on the bedroom to which she must flee with panic. But I mustn't hurry, she thought.

Seeing the unmade bed and herself lying in it face down like a suicide, she turned from it, half pretending she was here for something else. She went back to the kitchen, searching the room as she entered, as if for a ray of hope. But, deserted as it was after the hurried breakfast, everything pointed to those who were missing. She stood looking round. Everything seemed soiled and incomplete. She imagined other rooms fresh and bright – it is myself, she thought, and everything she saw confirmed this except the mahogany table, huge and solid, which seemed there in spite of herself. She sat bent a little forward, only her eyes moving. The stillness of the room began to affect her, so that her slightest movement seemed strange and somehow dangerous. The open window chilled her and she looked helplessly at it. She had a sense of constriction, of unnatural stillness from which she couldn't move. Not without something totally new from which she shrank afraid, overwhelmed. Then the cat came into the room and she felt a sudden relief. She waited, watching to see if he would come to her, and when he did she felt a sudden joy and remotely touched his head. But when she felt his fur she thought with an inward groan, I am glad to see a cat, and fell back upon the sofa. Hardly moving, she raised her legs and lay stiffly, as if she lay on stone. She felt better. She was doing something natural, she thought. She felt the silence and looked up to listen. Gradually it came – ringing, as if she held a shell to her ear – a timeless movement that dwarfed her and of which she knew nothing.

Two heavy bands seemed to close her eyes, and with great relief she decided to sleep. She felt her weight fall from her in a delicious current, becoming aware that the hand within her dress was clutched unnaturally. She imagined it exposed, attracting a pitying glance.

I must move, she thought, but her body was numb, and she felt it did not belong to her. Remembering how she must move she imagined legs swung down, but her own legs were immovable and in spite of her despair as she imagined their rigid appearance she felt no discomfort, and this gave her courage. This is their way, she thought defiantly. Her eyelids were still heavy on her eyes, yet it seemed to her there were cracks either side through which she could see. Her mind was all confusion over which memory turned, a mad machine, sometimes spurting sparks of fear and dread, yet always quickly carrying her on without a pause; a chain of memory marking time that must not stop and engulf her timelessly. With a great sigh she turned, half knowing the rhythm would start again. I do not think – she struggled desperately for clarity – these thoughts think me. Let me think of something – and love, love came, raising her up and beating down on her so that, gasping, she struggled to move and stood up.

There's that Ben, she thought, to bring herself back, liking what seemed the brave sound of her shoes. She must grind life, not give herself up to it and become, in its very radiance, hideous. In the years stretching inexorably ahead she would exist less and less unless she took his life in hers. She saw the clock. It was time to eat and she frowned. She thought of Rose and counted to four o'clock – I'll wait till she comes. Then thoughts came like a mass of pricking needles, overwhelming her. Her face crumpled as she felt the agony of distraughtness and saw Rose dart from beneath her raised arm. She turned and saw the next-door window through her own. What's going on there? she wondered, and such a presentiment of gloom and stillness, paralysing and consuming the small life within, came bowing her down that she lay again upon the sofa, looking fearfully up at the ceiling as if for the last time.

Hearing the door jarred by the wind, her fear made her imagine invincible murderers, but she knew at the same instant that this was only the last act. Unimportant, she had contracted out of life and felt relieved to put by hope, to blot it out in mediocre life like the bad colour of the stained carpet she lay on. She turned onto her stomach and entered into that state of total immobility in which she felt time stretch to aeons and form its rock over her, lying beneath it in subsistence.

She was awakened by a knock on the door which gave her a shock, twisting her face to unrelenting malignance, dilating and making terrible her eyes. She went to the mirror to tidy her hair, forcing her face to lift with little prancing movements of her mouth; and from her came a cracked note as she made an effort to sing.

It's from over the road, she thought suddenly. She's gone. She hurried to the door, feeling rise within her the awe and greatness of death.

Her first look was across the road at the blinds, then her eyes leapt at the young man who stood afraid, knowing he was beaten. 'Aye! Again! What is it?' she threatened with irritation, her eyes leaping at him, then receding.

'The bill.' The boy cringed, and almost broke down.

She gave out a long wordless cry, flapping her hand to shoo him away. 'Don't come here with your bills!' she screamed, her eyes bulging as her voice rose. For a moment she stood, a burning, living, gargoyle, then she suddenly softened to a terrible malignance. 'Tell us about the new motorbike instead!' she said, returning his confidence with ghastly mockery. 'The one you're buying and where the money's coming from – I know and we all know!' Everything in her seemed to suddenly leap out at him, so that he backed away. 'And I'll tell him' – her voice rose – 'the manager I mean – sending bits of boys like you – tell him to come!' she screamed, flinging her arm. 'And don't let me find you on this doorstep again!' She stood for a moment transfixed with passion, her arm raised as if to curse, vibrating like a mighty ringing bell. Her eyes swept over the neighbouring houses – so completely forgotten they seemed suddenly strange. Convinced she was being watched, that all was being recorded, she felt condemned, and with her head low re-entered the house.

As she walked down the passage she felt she was reeling, and closed her eyes. She felt she was longing for the answer to a terrible question, and prayed for pity from she knew not where. Entering the room she wondered, amazed, what had happened, and she looked afraid. She had been so quiet, so weak, yet all that fire suddenly. Where from? Hidden within her. Hidden! She half-imagined a cancerous growth, then sudden faint thumps of her heart made her feel herself to be sinister. Afraid of herself, she turned quickly, pushing these thoughts from her, and moved about the room. She cleared dishes from the table, and as if taking fresh heart looked at each part of the room, quickly calculating the work to be done. Gasping as if in sudden pain she saw work lay everywhere. In a great hurry she tidied the room, committed by slovenliness to depths beneath her, then went towards the parlour, pausing with big round solemn eyes as she turned the handle.

There was silence here, but in the red and gold of the room a different silence, alive like that of a church. Mrs Donald stood still, then touched the magnificent table. She looked slowly round, her look becoming fierce, then she moved, giving small touches here and there.

About to leave the room her eyes were drawn to the huge, beautiful portrait of herself which she had avoided. She saw first what seemed to her to be imperfections, then looked at the gentle appealing smile, the huge solid roundness of the jaw and felt the ghost of a stab as though from agony passed.

# Chapter 13

Walking to school Rose followed reverently behind an immaculate child, gazing at the exquisite freshness of the bare skin which she recognised at once and which she knew continued beneath the skirt all over. How long does it take? she wondered. She imagined, but quickly suppressed, the luxurious lapping of water, caressing, pampering a careless white leg. She set herself gigantic tasks involving weeks and years of washing her legs from the very top – and seeing herself doing this one leg steaming above the tiny bowl, the picture toppled. For an instant she saw whiteness, softness, tender hands against a white dress. She wrenched herself from looking up into a gentle face and saw brown, grey; the dirty steaming bowl and dungeons wherever she darted her eyes. Bursting into a run as if defeated by a drumming she had heard all along – It is always, always, and everything, she cried within.

Captivated, she watched friends calling, rushing across the playground to meet, their arms locking, they eyes searching, their equality beautiful. These were exalted. She felt overcome and ashamed looking down upon Ivy craven-faced with subjection.

As the warning bell sounded she leapt with all her might, with fantastic speed, in huge bounds round the playground, touching with a great cry objects normally far beyond her reach, followed now by a chain of children. Their boundless energy, freedom and natural grace caused a prick of envy in the staff who saw.

Towards the end of the school day Rose became silent and heavy with unconscious dread. Then, despair gently overwhelming her like sleep, she felt nothing, so that she woke with relief to find herself at home; standing before the sink in silence, her mother quiet. She looked back through the way she must have come, and felt a danger was over. She looked down upon her work and lifted her face in a burst of silent glorification – I will do it for you – I will do it for you. The work was difficult and unpleasant, with only cold hard water to remove the grease, and when a plate was clean her hand would glide round and round it while she looked up at the window full of the peace and the atmosphere of order it brought. Then slowly, dazed, numbed, she worked automatically.

'Aye! Look at her, the creeping Jesus. Is she all there? I ask you! Aye, wipe your feet!' shouted Mrs Donald to Lennie who had entered the house. 'And wipe that look off your face or I'll do it for you. You're getting too big for your boots m'lad, you want a man behind you!' As he went through to the yard with his bike, Mrs Donald felt new blood stir within her, and she moved around the room, busy. Rose brought cups and saucers into the kitchen, standing stupidly holding onto the tray.

'Come on!' cried her mother, her finger moving as if to dig at her, and then, pointing to the sink, 'Clean as a new pin I want it and it hasn't been touched, I lay, then there's the floors upstairs – come on!' she cried, before Rose could droop, 'You're old enough and ugly enough!' As she saw the child's back she felt sorry for Rose, but she would be rid of her and the work had to be done. 'Aye!' she cried to crush her guilt. 'Upstairs first – and don't forget I'll be up to look under the beds!' She felt the necessity to dispense with Rose, whose innocence seemed to perfect her guilt, whose very terror seemed her natural prey, the very lamb on which she leapt like a tiger.

Rose climbed the stairs like a cripple, in agony at every step, her mouth stretched wide and her head constantly weaving until her convulsed throat, swelled and constricted, relaxed in a dreadful sob.

'And here comes another one!' said Mrs Donald as she watched Freddie come towards her. 'Look at him! Out there and wash!' she screamed, her arm flung. He passed her quickly. 'Aye!' She stopped him with hideous malice as he turned. 'And don't be afraid of the water!'

Her face worked with disgust as she occasionally glimpsed him. His shoulders were hunched and his grey working shirt clung, wrinkled, to the hollows between. His movements were quickened with fear, his cupped hands moving over the soap as if frantic to start. She felt his washing was pointless. He could never be clean. Tormented by a loathing she could never express, she said, as if to Lennie, 'Did you hear about the sausages on Saturday? The dirty tyke!' Then, seeing him cringe, watching openly, helplessly for her next move, she felt it beneath her to notice him further. She turned, her eyes rolling upward as an unconscious thought arrested her. She strained for an instant to decipher a whisper. Then, grateful for calmness – the embodiment of that which she felt had escaped her, for the tumult she had avoided which moment-arily moved in quick agony through her, she closed her eyes and breathed deeply, and felt she breathed a new air. She walked to her bedroom with a heady sense of worlds at her fingertips, a feeling that she could leave all unpleasantness behind, and idly choose. She closed the door as if to preserve this feeling. To be alone, she thought, looking up. She saw herself in a little boat, a silhouette on a wide dark sea, slowly rocked towards a far horizon. Then she saw her children's

76

eyes become the round hard eyes of birds – unknowing, unfeeling, on guard – holding her at bay while their limbs and jaws were driven to tear by a terrible energy that nothing could stop. Horrified, she shuddered and buried her head on her arm, and without feeling saw herself standing as she was now, forever in the same place, gradually falling to pieces, her only comfort closing her eyes.

When she moved at last she felt overwhelmingly humble, the servant of everything she saw, and found consolation and identity as she tidied the room.

'Is that you, Billy?' she called, as if from a sick bed, hearing him slowly walking through the house. Then quickly leaving the room she saw his tall back at the kitchen door. All her hope and very lifestream seemed to flow from her towards him. She felt she had been released from wandering and was now on a path that led to overwhelming peace. A mother, she told herself. To put herself aside . . . Her eyes closed and a great weariness left her. To be always behind him, watching over his need – to resign herself. She saw herself, bowed by sacrifice, in a background of shadows; a broken figure in faded blue but inured to pain.

Watching him slowly eating, day-dreaming, she felt the enormous distance between them. She wondered what ab-sorbed him and felt he was weaving his future which would surround him with glowing light and radiant faces. But no one ever mentions the mother, she thought. She spoke to him disjointedly, asking after his day in sad comforting tones, consoling herself.

'My brother Tom came to see me today,' she said, turning from him. Billy looked at her for the first time, too disgusted to speak. He examined her from top to toe then pushed his food away in distaste.

'What's the matter?' she asked, turning with a haunted

look. 'What's the matter?' she demanded as he rose.

'What d'you want to say that for? Lies –!' His face and voice were pained. 'The lies you tell – it's disgusting!'

'Aye! I'll give you disgusting! My brother Tom was here today!' she said imperiously, pointing into the room. 'And get out –!' she cried as he moved to the door. 'All the slommocks and corner boys are waiting for you, I lay – a disgrace to the neighbourhood.'

'And one day I'll stay out!' he muttered.

'Aye, and then you'll miss your mother!' she cried triumphantly. 'And when I'm dead and gone – none of us lasts for ever – least of all your mother who has had to work her fingers to the bone – to be mother and father to the lot of you – I shan't be sorry when my time comes! Don't bring sorrow to *my* grave!'

No one listened to her words but at the sound of her voice, which rose and rose like the sea gathering strength, there was general caution which she felt as hostility. She felt a terrible misery swiftly devouring her strength, and looked wildly up, then flung out her arms. 'Look at the home I keep for a lot of tykes who belong to the workhouse or the gallows. Where they'd beeee!' – her voice pierced and rang – 'the whole lot of them but for their mother!' In one soft bound she was at the door he had closed upon her. 'Kids!' she shrieked, demented by his escape. 'Why do we have them! Why don't we all swing for them!'

The front door banged and she felt her cries fall round her in the empty room, and silence descending. Her eyes, like dazzling blue lights, rolled, tragic and helpless, over the room to where, at the windows, she imagined her neighbours waiting, breathless. Then she saw Freddie at the scullery door.

He had stood flattening himself against the wall, ready at

the first sign of a lull to pop his head in, say something and leave, and when the door banged he felt he had missed his moment. In the silence he faced her, clutching the wall to speed him away, his eyes bolting in their effort to look at her.

A majestic sense of her great suffering rose within her as she saw him so miserably afraid. She lifted her eyes above his head and in the act of fleeing he was arrested by the spectacle of her face.

Alone in the room she turned her lofty solemn head. I suffer – she told herself – if ever woman did. She saw herself martyred, a spotless vision in the sky, and dropped her head wearily as the vision discoloured, blacking out from the heart. But will they think so? she thought bitterly, and felt another burden pressed upon her. Closing her eyes, grateful for darkness, she felt life ebbing – as if drawn from her by some swift anaesthetic. Gratefully she met the oncoming blackness which she felt overwhelming her.

# Chapter 14

Violet went to meet Louis. Closing her eyes as she entered the crowded pub she felt that the compulsion that brought her to meet him must end in stunning collision. As soon as she saw him she opened her mouth, laughing; her words all laughter to break the force of their meeting. 'Terribly funny –!' she began, seeing everything as comic, as he did, and telling him brilliantly of her radiant progress through the outside world to which they didn't belong – didn't belong.

'Wonderful.' He laughed back at her, fetching their drinks. It was her health that was so wonderful, he reminded himself again. 'Do you know how I can tell you are really young?' he teased. 'Because the whites of your eyes are blue!'

He watched her, wondering at how she changed. She contained, he felt, dynamos of energy which if released would lift him from his chair, and he almost put out his hand to rise. She was beautiful, he told himself, but she would never know it so nothing would come of it. Young though she was, he felt she was caught. There was a hint of defeat in the way she sat, as if the self she saw was doomed to the indifference of the world, was the palpable embodiment of submission. He gave her the book of poems he had promised to bring.

'I met a woman today who said she had time taped,' he said, delighted. She looked away, afraid. 'Good, don't you think?' he asked, bored because she hid her face, now watching her, openly challenging. At this she fled to the lavatory. She opened the book of poems. Inside he had written from L. to V. and the date, but – no love, no love, death-knelled in her mind, the echo of her own denial. She came down the stairs into the crowd and noise, feeling she would never find him. She pushed past heads and shoulders in an agony of knowing she had no contact with him, or with the great world represented here, which he carried in his head. Their eyes met in fear, longing for closer contact, and they got out.

'I don't make love to you enough,' he said. 'Shall I take a room?'

'No!' she said, with a definiteness he always trusted; and yet it might be romantic if they did. She raised her mind's eye and saw, standing in that room, the great lovers they might become. But as she stood in his arms her eye fell on dust which lay everywhere like a bloom over all colour and lustre. The room was lifeless, could belong to no one, its void seeping into the void between them. And now this whole part of London seemed fiery with ideas, none of which she could understand. Her feet striking the pavement led where she would not go, and seemed like her own head striking and obtaining no response. The sound reverberated in her mind like pain from a dream world. But from the outside she chatted to him gaily, imagining the tall house they went towards, and Dinah standing there waiting for their coming.

They entered the house – turning like strangers from each other – simultaneously aware of this like bed-rock between them; embarrassed, they climbed the stairs.

Dinah rose. Her loneliness like famine in the room. 'The girl with the dark brown voice!' she greeted her.

Violet turned insolently, as if she had rights there, was become the condescending mistress, looking critically about while Dinah watched, avoiding the eyes which made her feel she had been discovered in the grave. Violet went to the window, turning her back like a cloud over the sun, from which her intensity streamed in rays.

'Don't ever change,' Louis implored, getting their drinks. She laughed, wondering how she looked, making a mental note of the clothes she wore. She saw her yellow hair nestled in her neck and softly gleaming as her mother's did; but, turning, she felt he had passed sentence on her, had doomed her to be as lifeless as these walls – implacably unchanging, and adumbrating overwhelming death. All three sat. Dinah, as though she was an umpire, between them. Louis settled down to complete relaxation, as he only could with someone there. He smiled at Vi, drawing looks from her eyes, light-hearted, gay and teasing, while she responded, delighted by his vulnerability, dangling herself before him to see him tremble.

'How's Johnny?' he began. 'Oh darling, do tell us!'

With looks of sweet intimacy which told him she had discovered his taste for stories, Vi told him everything that had happened since they had last met, conceiving everything as funny for the first time, throwing all her energy into amusing him; his attention a spotlight forcing her on.

Dinah saw Violet laughing now in the blaze of his attention which held her poised as if for sacrifice, enthralled by siren songs in which she watched her dying. She looked along her mind to inviolate privacy where Louis lurked, like Cerberus in the dark, eyes closing upon herself – the crucial evil, the hideous beldam who had found his ravine. But she knew, relieved, it was more than this, an agony she could not explain. She tried to see into Louis's inexplicable relations with people – his incapacity to relate to them which she knew so well by instinct and which showed Louis to her like a child whom it would be irrelevant to blame.

She watched Louis, smiling life racing through him, vivid

with success in work, in fame of which Vi mirrored back the proof.

'You've got a rough nose!' he teased Violet gaily, eyes fixed on hers as he drew her in to give up to him, gasping all her secrets. 'All girls who don't get kissed have rough noses – now then!' he looked to Dinah, kissing her, remembering it was she who had found her for him, there was so much to enjoy – so much to enjoy – because she was here turning all her light upon him. Things must always be like this, and special for him, Dinah knew. Her eyes closed upon herself and every other claim in which the drama of his greatness leapt and widened! He was indeed the light of the world while she hovered over him, living for a day. And what else would she do, Dinah asked herself, ice-cold, conscious he had touched her and driven iron in.

'Poor Johnny!' Vi sighed as Louis rose to fetch their drinks. 'You should have seen his arm on the sofa, edging by inches towards me!' and she was carried away, as she saw it, by her own vitality which rose in great gouts from the madness of being here, the hideous knowledge that she was completely cut off, could receive no sustenance, must spin out whatever life was left, or life itself would come to an end. Throwing herself bodily to span the abyss she felt her senses leave her as she worked herself up until her words, all laughter, seemed to come of their own momentum. For that was what she was here for. The thought came like pain from the effort, swooped like a dying bird over her mind.

Louis looked to Dinah in complete submission, his face giving way as their eyes met. 'No one ever laughed like that,' he said. Vi rose, a little tipsy, to go to the bathroom, ridiculing, as she went, the neighbours opposite, who in delicious reflection of the glamour here she called 'the drears'. Outside she sagged as if after a terrible performance. Her eyes searched the walls. It all seemed alien and she was here in the dereliction of no man's land, but she felt them like demons in that room, the accumulating silence compelling her return.

Louis looked to Dinah half-fearfully as if to divine what she felt, gauging her as though he was a child, for the word go – then careless of this, gave himself over to exultation, his eye bright with knowing that life could not be otherwise than as he wished, and that now, transcending, he would take it by the hand. Dinah gasped, ideas half-formed collapsing on her mind. She saw Louis smiling, escaped and free, his life un-circumscribed, and envy seized her like a fiend. She saw that Louis would go, take all – even his own familiar self – and leave her powerless.

'Darling,' Louis said, rising to meet Vi as she returned. 'I do love you!' he said helplessly. Violet smiled and sat on his lap, balancing herself across him as if he were there entirely for her convenience, her skirt falling fan-like – looking to-wards Dinah whose admiration gave her greater freedom. She turned full upon Louis, watching his lip tremble, laugh-ing at his complete submission. She knew she had only to look deep into his eyes to discover and expose him, but at this she sickened and gently made fun of him while he stroked her neck, feeling the little warts there like thorns on a rose.

'I do love you,' he said helplessly again.

'You don't yet, but you will!' She threw back her head, dismissing him. 'You don't yet but you will!' she said again, watching it happen while Louis watched her eyes, in which her future loomed and came towards her in bright apoth-eosis.

He turned to Dinah and they saw her, like failure, stalking them. In the circle she wove round herself they were left outside. Louis couldn't forgive her the feeling she showed – it was as though his own familiar were cheating him, and from that moment would be cut off from him. He frowned furiously, caught out like a child in his own irrelevance.

As Dinah rose to go to bed she felt her own position strangely fixed. She felt the circle of her own movements like a small sphere outside of which was giddy space, terrible powers she preferred not to know – from which, as she wrenched her head familiarly away, anathema would fall. This was the great enemy, and, strengthened, she was glad to be reminded. She put her hand to the wall, blinding herself until the moment passed. But her mind ranged over what seemed a constant vigil. From whence came the mysterious justice of life, that ominous remote order which seemed always to threaten them? The laughable idea of a supreme being, arms stretched over the world, was, when faced, an abhorrent insult. Clearing her throat of a grossness which must be admitted but dismissed, she knew life itself was the enemy with its hideous necessity – its ultimate horror of birth and death. She felt herself rescued from wordless mystery, standing calmly in sunlight, while behind her were savage caves. Looking towards them to say goodnight she knew it was here that she was at one with Louis.

When she left they tumbled to the floor. Vi lived so much in his need that she gave herself up to him, turning from her own revulsion, giving herself gladly up to the violence which seemed like the wreaking out of all that had gone before. But she must be beautiful for him, she told herself aghast, relieved as she saw she must be so in a splendour of extremity on the floor.

When he left her on the train she envied him his quiet walk home, recollected and alone, while she, as she turned to pull herself together, found her centre gone, and flew in all directions.

# Chapter 15

In the Church Hall, hidden by a group of girls, each pressing to get closer, Miss Benson sat sewing. Before her, stretched at ease, lay Rose, on whom all twinkling eyes were turned, visibly waiting. Rose felt she lay on scales which she could tip this way or that to bring blushes or confusion to Miss Benson.

'If we all come from Adam and Eve how did it happen, Miss!' she asked for their amusement.

Miss Benson's head rose automatically towards Mr Matthews as if she'd watched him all along.

'Why don't you get married, Miss?' said Rose, following her gaze. 'Would you like to?' she asked agreeably, with mocking probing eyes on wounded longing. 'And have a baby?' she added thickly, becoming lost in the great blush that transformed Miss Benson. Rose looked up at cheeks made round and tender. 'You love him, don't you?' she cried, her malice gone. Miss Benson got up, a swarm of children moving with her. 'You love him, don't you?' they cried, delighted by her succumbing smile.

The children sat in serried rows and Mr Matthews began to teach from the Bible. Mavis, Ivy and Rose, in the best seats, did not listen. Elaborately whispering and giggling, they studied the creased fork of his trousers, looking from this place with guarded flashes into his eyes to show him they were well aware of the wickedness he hid. Rose became fascinated by his blue eye, which was so open and appealing, yet behind which so much evil must be hidden.

Gradually inclining his head as he spoke, he seemed to her suddenly a sick man, expiring, yet with his last breath calling them with the gentlest patience. Rising to sing she saw her heart as a drift of snow but with black melted spots, never to be clean. As they burst, howling, into the street Rose saw her home as the final grey path that ended in blackness. Along its sides faint rainbow mists of everything else she knew collapsed and faded like dreams. She closed her eyes, forgetting. About to say goodnight, she remembered her evil behaviour and suddenly saw that in the darkness of home retribution lay in wait, a monster that heaved as she watched. With a shriek she fled to the wall. Her frantic eyes pretending that she played, she went onwards alone, her head thrown back, imploring for another chance, her eyes closed with great longing as she saw herself next Wednesday – docile, gentle and sweet. Goldenhaired, sitting in blue and white, she added in reckless despair. Her knees often giving way in terror that made her almost sink to the ground, she reached the main road, lurching away from the glimpse it gave. Stepping onto the cobbles words fell from her. Running, she prayed, in agony, helplessly. She suddenly saw that her prayers were useless because she only prayed in terror, and even now her lips were hidden in shame – but she prayed harder. Half-lifting her head in a supreme effort she wanted to start over again, as a saint, to make fresh promises, but she saw into her despised heart and could not. Running into her street, her eyes closed, her head averted as if she must rush into a great storm – she hurled herself forward, oblivious.

Moments later, alone in her room, which she reached without incident, she paused, looking gratefully up at the air around her, confidently surrounded by tenderness.

She woke slowly, bewildered in the night, apprehensively drawing together all her faculties to understand what had frightened her. She heard the sound of heavy breathing and felt the stroking, the trembling hand hardly touching her. She knew, as if she had seen him, that it was her brother, and saw at once that safety lay in pretending sleep; and imagining her eyes open and meeting his, in lifelong participation in this scene, knew she'd been saved. She made motions of waking and he fled stumbling. She lay rigid without moving, then slept.

# Chapter 16

The next day, excited by a knock on the door, Mrs Donald went to answer. Round and compact, she hurried buoyantly as if every bit of her felt the urgency to move; half-smiling, her tongue darting over his lips, she broke into song as she puzzled who could be there. As she drew back the door she involuntarily drew herself up, her eyes becoming dragon-like, collapsing into tragedy when she saw Mr Matthews. She drew him into the house with a chorus of cries seeming almost unconscious, delirious, except when she looked up at him. She was immensely solicitous, breaking into smiles of great warmth as he spoke to her in his Scotch accent.

'But how are you?' She opened her arms, amazed again to find him there. Alone in the scullery, she threw back her head, rocking it gently as she drew cups from their hooks. She felt a flow of warmth had come, taking her with it, and closing her eyes she felt she was waltzing.

'Mr Matthews,' she sighed, overwhelmingly content. 'Aye, I've got nothing for you!' she cried, aghast, the Saturday shopping flooding her mind.

She felt that she was incarcerated on an island and he came to her across seas, and thoughts overcharged by years poured, unconnected, from her. Through the helter skelter of her talk and the bewildering rush of her Mr Matthews sat looking up in a vague state of emergency, ready to speak, to answer.

She looked at him, taking fresh pleasure in his visit, her

smile becoming faintly mocking, amused, as she saw his interest in her. She felt she faced him remotely across a river which rushed like the present between them, and her only connection with the past would never be recaptured – like her youth.

Calmer, she almost forgot him. Looking into the fire, absorbed by memory, as if, safely anchored to him, she could visit scenes which otherwise would suck her down; her face changed and grimaced as if she watched events which she agonisingly understood, yet was finally awed by some great mystery. Talking, unconscious of what she said, the words falling from her in a steady flow seemed someone else's, and gave no glimpse of the inexpressible things she saw – as if this were not their purpose but came only as noise comes from a running stream. He felt he had lost her, that he could make no further impression, that this visit was after all only a sad endurance. Suddenly deafened by her words, a torrent rushing between them, he felt himself sinking, dazed, and made an effort to move.

He found it was easier to look at only one side of her face, which was divided like the mask on a theatre curtain. One side of it was round and sweet and his eyes continually darted from the other which fell, as if dragged down by paralysis; the unnatural eye vacant, or haunted. He was suddenly startled by the utter blackness which covered her face, his eyes slurring away as he saw her transfixed by bitter memory. Slowly recovering, she turned to him as if to forget that which loomed so large it seemed like madness in her eyes. She felt him plunge directly into her misery and, violated, reared herself away, turning herself from him.

She saw that behind all that she would not tell him, which she kept hidden like secret treasure – surprised he loomed so large – was her neighbour's husband, Ben. She fell again to her memories, though now carelessly, lifting an arm to hold back the overwhelming things she knew. Looking above his head then into his eyes as she spoke, her head falling and gently rocking on the back of her chair, she smiled and her face took on such dazzling innocence he could have fallen before her in relief.

Reminded of everyday life, bitter and despairing, she seemed suddenly to have done with everything; her eyes, half opening and closing, then rolling upward to the rhythm of her words, were like coverts where a thousand savages danced.

He looked down and saw her hands, which seemed innocent as they lay passive. He saw that something covered her in blackness, a slow disease which had not reached her hands, leaving them as terrible shreds of her beauty. Almost weeping with pity he wanted to kiss them, to fall on his knees.

'But me, I always forgive – always forgive,' she said as if these were her dying words, her eyes rolling upward as if giving up the ghost.

'But what about this Heath?' she asked suddenly, as if at last they could talk about something.

He glimpsed Rose passing the doorway, carrying part of the stove. 'I'm training her,' said Mrs Donald, rising decisively. It was about Rose he had called and he spoke of her. Mrs Donald raised her arm, her hand exaggeratedly poised as if in mime. 'I want interference from no one!' she said, on her guard, all intimacy gone. Her feelings rushed like rivers inside her. She felt chaos rising, bowling her over, and to hold it off forced herself to speak. She saw with great calm that he was only a boy.

'There's only one way to bring up children,' she said with disregard. 'You see this?' She pointed to a cane above her head. 'Chastisement!' she cried, her eyes leaping at the word.

Rose heard his gentle murmur swept away.

'That's all very well for some people,' cried Mrs Donald, 'but not for widows left with five of them to scrape and save. Spare the rod and spoil the child!' Her voice rose. 'You've heard of that, I suppose,' she added, calmed by the insult.

'Won't you stay and see Lennie?' she asked, looking up at him as he rose. Putting money into an envelope, she licked it with satisfaction. 'I'll be there next Sunday,' she said, smiling tearfully, comforted by sudden hope.

She looked round the street as she said goodbye, proud of him at her side, graciously smiling upon all, naively identifying with his importance.

Mr Matthews walked down the street, estranged from himself in the thought of her. She was like a problem increased beyond the pale of reason which would respond to nothing less than exorcism. I must think of her – I must think of her. He threw himself into it. And I must make a plan for Rose.

Returning to the kitchen to prepare the evening meal, Mrs Donald mused upon Rose, looking apprehensively at the child's back which was turned towards her as she stood at the sink, her eyes puckering as if expecting to see something unpleasant. She noticed the strong muscles in the back of the child's neck, which stood out – so palpable and individual she wanted to crush them between finger and thumb. Vividly she saw there the child's will and vision scheming as she watched. She saw monstrous deceit in the bent head that tossed itself high outside the house. For an excruciating moment she glimpsed Rose away from home, proud and unafraid. Frustration that the child sometimes escaped her thrilled her with insufferable impotence right through to her sex. She wanted to scourge the white skin – to burn it – her eyes closed upon a delirium of images of the terrible vulnerability of the flesh.

She looked at the innocent unsuspecting back, which seemed so terribly exposed, patiently, unconsciously immersed in work, and a mass of inklings stirred in her mind, overwhelming her. She gradually saw Rose as a complete whole from whom her own thoughts receded, an absolute that could not cease to be. Feeling herself fall under an influence Mrs Donald felt afraid and moved uneasily. She saw the clock and, relieved, hurried on with her arrangement of the table in which she took such pride.

Lennie came in, breaking off a piece of tart as he passed the table wheeling his bike.

'Aye, I do believe it was him had the sausages on Saturday!' Mrs Donald cried fiercely.

'Why should I touch them?' he said, unconcerned, with an omniscient glance into the scullery at Rose.

His mother's eye darted after his look and felt that the truth was dawning at last.

'Aye!' she cried into the scullery. 'Look at her! Sly as they make them,' she muttered aside at the mock innocent girl, and pointed to a spot before her to which Rose slowly came. 'The sausages on Saturday,' said Mrs Donald, her face contorting with the sensual pleasure of being both polite and deadly.

Rose became guilty red, then pale; her arms dropped slowly, stiffly to her sides. For a moment she seemed hypnotised, huge appeal in her eyes. Her lips moved in an effort to speak then, despairing, she raised her white face.

Mrs Donald was so struck she turned from it and noticed instead the trembling lip like a full drop of water about to fall. As she paused she saw the child weighing her chances and loathing sprang up in her. She saw Rose ill-dressed, scarred by her nails, and miserable. Knowledge of the child's every degradation came into Mrs Donald's execrating look, at which Rose's eye half leapt with terror then glazed with shame. Raising her hand as if to strike she mocked the flinching child with such contempt that Rose, annihilated, backed out of the room.

Dropping into a chair Mrs Donald felt weary, unhappy. She wanted Billy to come so that her day would end. And there's Violet, she thought. Where are they all?

'You're late,' she said, rising and looking at the clock as Billy appeared. She put his meal before him with a guilty look. 'There's not much for your dinner! I haven't had five minutes to myself all day – and I never know when they'll be coming for me from over the road. Aye, move over!' she cried at Lennie. He moved with weary disgust and she eyed him threateningly as he passed her, leaving the room.

While Billy ate she turned away to the fire, her eyes occasionally peering malignantly through to the dim scullery at Rose, who bolted back to work.

'Look at her! Sly as they make them,' said Mrs Donald. Very soon Billy pushed his plate from him.

'What's the matter with it?' she asked, frowning. 'My legs have been bad all day,' she added with sudden weakness.

'Have they?' he asked with attentive surprise, his voice so soft and gentle it seemed to come from another world, far off, serene. She looked at him with longing. He sat slumped forward, his head raised stiffly over his plate, putting bread and butter into his mouth with slow clockwork movements.

An inoffensive lad, she thought, feeling stir within her a deep well from which she caught a dark gleam.

'Mr Matthews was here today,' she said quickly. 'About that one in there,' she added with malignance. 'She's been up to something, not that we will ever know what it is.'

'Tea, Ma?' said Billy.

'Tea!' she screamed. 'Is that all you think about? Must we

all be murdered in our beds before you'd stir? You'd do better to ask after your mother for once and liven yourself up a bit!'

As he rose stoically she realized with hysteria that she'd been shouting again. Aghast and trembling she saw herself as a river in spate or a bolting horse. She saw that Mr Matthews had identified this. She felt excitement as though some great cerebral wave was teaching her to think, to possess herself in reason and dispossess the madness that howled like dogs within her, and she turned to hold herself in check.

# Chapter 17

Louis, preparing to leave, was saying his farewells. He looked at Violet from where he stood at the bar, chatting to friends. To take her, so brilliantly new, to the party they were off to seemed a head-on clash of past and future. She wasn't properly dressed and now, as she felt his scrutiny, hardly in a party mood. She had no claims, he reminded himself, remembering the mutually embarrassed glance in which countless times he had put up barriers like a stretch of private ground between them. A void seemed to open up and carry him downstairs.

Violet instinctively felt his attitude, and felt herself stiffening. He would go now, she thought, and leave her there. She longed to move the great weight in her bones but felt as though she were made of clay which would crack if she moved. It was like those evenings after a marvellous time which they knew instinctively could not be repeated, and they fled from what was lacking between them. She felt him sail away, even now, on the ship. She would not feel, she must not care, only accept – quietly pretend that this was normal. She would not go into it, she would avoid the issue, and the agony would surge away – dreamlike.

He went over and talked to her, sustained by Dinah, who he saw between them as a natural barrier. Their words took on another meaning as they spoke. She glimpsed his experience and felt outside it, holding on to her bitterness with which she might torture him. He saw, disburdened, the vision he'd painted, the essence of her he'd got down on canvas, and now the substance undisguised, her face primeval, dark, with eyes like knives denying all he knew. She was so much more revealed, had forever escaped him, and now he felt he'd bypassed truth to capture dreams. He had longed to look beyond what he immediately saw, to discard what had formed in his mind, to see that which he had feared to probe. But he had got down what he knew, he told himself, as his vision, highly wrought, came to him, capping all.

'Leave me here,' she said. 'I am expecting someone.' She could bear it, but only alone. She could not get up now and stumble out with him.

'I will send a postcard,' said Louis quickly, off to the party as if to present life to live, the knowledge that he might have taken her visible in their eyes, the final moment ceasing to exist except in nightmare regions. Dinah, watching, knew this was better than those long-drawn-out endings when they seemed to walk – oh, for ages – with the dead. Following Louis, Dinah and Violet turned to each other for that necessity of understanding, as if forever wedded; the consciousness between them outweighing all. In the question, large but unspeakable, of what was to his advantage they saw the danger. The future might even bring lawyers, like bogeymen, on the horizon. Then smiling, boy-like, Louis hurried with a gay conception of whole new futures into which he felt himself advance deliciously, as if he'd been cooped up. The ordinary mortal Dinah, looking up, saw the guilt, its threatening shapes contorting them, and Louis, like a child possessed, as if he were, in turn, the victim. She felt she must oppose, protest, hold up her arms as if to ward off blows. She saw Louis look to her in sickness, felt his awful weight devolve as something failed, and he subsided into her.

Violet looked down the long bar, surprised she had never done this before, half aware that many people sat as she did, aimlessly alone, and that she was in no immediate danger of notice. Descending the stairs she knew she would never go home, and realised belatedly that home had never existed. The agony of being responsible for herself rose quickly and she was aware of herself as an awful encumbrance. Living for herself would be non-existence. She wished only to place herself very low, be caught up in some organisation — a hospital, perhaps, become anonymous. But even there she would have to be herself, would have to look into the eyes of people, and her look would be like a shock from which they would both reel. A thin blade in her two hands, piercing her chest to tear out the agony there, would be truer and infinitely better.

The long stooping form of Johnny appeared and her mind lurched away. Her eyes switched quickly to his hands, which she liked. She could tell herself she loved him while looking into his eyes, she could fall, as it were, into this bed of oblivion until, quietly, her senses could live in this time. The vision arose of Louis at sea — her last certain picture of him. Here she would keep vigil, and here the deep undercurrents of her mind would flow and all that was herself would be suppressed.

She went out to a telephone box, raised the phone and spoke to Louis.

'I will tell Johnny!' she said, the menace and huge implication of her words gripping beyond reason.

'He won't believe you,' Louis said, forcing her back, his awareness taut like a knife at his throat.

In a vision of the world over which Louis presided, of the circle in which he moved, among friends who existed within themselves in an equilibrium which omitted her, she saw great customs to which she must conform, silent demands she must meet. She must join the conspiracy in the hooded eye of each whited sepulchre.

She put down the phone knowing that only one thing mattered, steeling herself to view it, raw and terrible. It was the protection Johnny would give her, the weekly income which would see her through. She comforted herself that Louis was safe. How she would have joyed to have given herself to him, be forgiven, excused, rejoice that they could now turn and carry on normally. Leaving the telephone box she swam in a featureless sea, alien to her, and of little concern except that it meant she had to keep her head above water. She saw, as if watching her own death, that he would never know or want to know – except cruelly, in passing. It was as if these were events within his mind, and not part of the great world in which he moved and in which, frightened, she saw she had no place. She did not dare look to where his view of her streamed, annihilated by her shame and his knowledge of it. But she was aware of what seemed a great emergency – she must shut out Johnny, hold him at bay, show him any face but her own, which, as she raised it, seemed a constellation half-unmade, reduced to pill size to marry him.

Louis put down the phone, the idea uppermost that he would be away, removed, the past in darkness like the dead. He remembered distinctly that not a word had been said, raising omnisciently the largest implication which he knew immediately would be the worst. But it was also all a question like countless others surrounding him imperceptibly; he must be unaware, draw back from what would drag him down. He was required to do nothing by law. These things worked themselves out in complexities and mutations through which life was extended as if into other worlds already humming with communication and moving, like himself, towards him.

# Chapter 18

When Violet did not come back Mrs Donald knew she had left. The world took on a new sound describing vast emptiness.

In a brilliant moment of sweet, normal worry she felt she should set enquiries afoot, but she shrank from the exposure as darkness overtook her, and there opened within a deep chasm of fear. Descending guilty depths she saw herself, with terrible justice, struck down by her own hand. She felt a terrible past resuscitated – the truth of judgement day, which she had always feared, was to be revealed like a curtain rising, and she moved, unable to endure. She closed her eyes, voided her mind so as not to see that that which she denied existed together with her own existence. There rose up within her a great silent cry, a repudiation of all else.

She was terrified that even now she could take some action, make some terrible act of contrition, and so find more to repent of until she was utterly crushed.

She remembered how when her Friday housework was done her husband had come, seeming to soil the place.

But she had come to know *him*, she soothed her mind, to know him intimately in terrible privacy through the child. It was all she did know, had ever thought about or was familiar with. It was as if they met in an underworld blotting all out in life. Without him her thoughts raged in oblivion – in anaesthesia in which she could indulge her passion.

It always seemed to her that for him there had been many such as her and that therefore her imaginings must be false, but as she said so she saw him look to her for vital recognition, their eyes with points like pinnacles in which they were personified. With a desperate need to make a move of her own, the simple need to talk denied past bearing, she saw the doomed insanity of her mind because she had no friends to believe in her. Raising her head she saw herself struggling within her bowed and monstrous shape, and saw with terror the desperate necessity to inveigle Ben into marriage.

She saw with strange fear that she had not realized it before, that Mr Matthew's concern had been about Rose, and with a horrible sense that he knew all about her, that nothing was hid, and that Violet leaving now had exposed her to the world, she told herself she would go to the school. She closed her eyes upon a tumultuous blackness as if to die and raise herself again, all sweetness, forcing hope to rise in little billows round her head.

She felt her soft clean hair and obliquely decided to go that day. She felt cunning wake behind her own closed eyes which, like sleeping dogs, must lie. She felt the power of her master-strokes and moved with care. The day was transformed from just being Thursday into an adventure which alarmed and excited her.

Leaving the house she walked with self-importance down the little street until she reached the main road where, making sure she had everything, she raised her head, full of naive hope and benediction; glad as she envisaged the route of long straight streets along which she could plunge, forgetting.

She would tell them her story, and pathos rose artlessly in her blue eyes which, raised in pity, saw her words a spangled web, she herself dark and sinister beneath.

When she saw Miss Benson she hurried comically, arms out as if to embrace her goal.

'Miss Benson came to see me when my husband died!' she said to Mr Matthews, moved by the woman's youth. 'You must come again!' Mrs Donald's voice was soft and calm and she dropped her eyes to force back tears, her courage draining from her as she raised them to Mr Matthews as if to a strong light in which she felt her senses leave her deaf and dumb and blind; a sheer monstrosity, turning, leaving herself for dead.

'This is a lovely room!' she said, forcing herself to speak. Her delight in the room was so great that she felt it was a solemn achievement to be there, and she looked back upon days of emptiness, gently defeating them. Ravenously, she imagined this room to be hers, and saw herself always sitting here, closed around with an ideal life. They watched her as they would a lovely bird who might open shattering wings, wonder-stricken and tremorous at each turn she gave.

'I'm glad you have come to see us,' said Mr Matthews. 'We are pleased with Rose, a promising and good girl.'

'She comes from a good home!' said Mrs Donald savagely. 'Miss Benson here can testify to that. And she's given every chance!' she added, as her eyes rolled with a mad glimmer of white, which Miss Benson hurriedly effaced from memory. 'A good home and good teachers!' she cried, dragging herself wearily over weary ground, now unconnected with her life. 'What more can she ask for?'

'But look at you!' said Mrs Donald to Miss Benson, overflowing with pity for this innocent who didn't yet know what age was. She anticipated the half-death blow this girl would feel, felt what sisters they could be when that time came, forgiving life as she lifted it – a double burden.

'You've got a rough nose!' she cried, gaily teasing. 'It hasn't been kissed enough – all girls who don't get kissed have rough noses. Now then!' she cried like a huge impresario, her arms out, inviting their helpless agreement.

When Miss Benson left their eyes crossed smoothly like two searchlights and each saw the other perfectly.

'It was in the war,' Mr Matthews was saying, recollected in that time. 'All that suffering, and none of it touching me, so I made a vow!'

Mrs Donald saw her future in his eye, profoundly understood his amused disinterest as he spoke of himself in passing. Looking towards a deeper confidence he saw that she too would come to know so that she would be able to bear no more of what he said – yet these were but minor details of a knowledge she would come to know, excruciatingly, by heart.

'I want Rose to go away,' she said with desperate hope, feeling it was not herself who spoke, but a stranger to whom she must give life and bring forth. She watched herself disappear with numb tongue, and the desolation of mere survival, bereft, half-paralysed. And with this blow others seemed to echo in the future. Mr Matthews watched Mrs Donald go – moving with her, before her – in unison with her needs, his familiar senses darkened, blind, limited in the great world to that within his reach, and lonely with secrets never to be divulged. He knew his own unspeakable darkness and felt himself descend into obliterating truth, repudiating that for which he always secretly longed – the only utterly complete sweetness of death. He saw himself arraigned to answer this one charge, beside which all his other sins, monstrous though they were, were trifles.

Mrs Donald walked quickly, thinking about Rose, receiving her as a sudden weight as she knew that Mr Matthews received her. She held her arms out in her first true act, raising her eyes to that great pearl, her consciousness, through which she saw and knew what she did.

# Chapter 19

The next afternoon Rose looked up as if recovering from sudden concussion. The playground around her, a mass of flying legs and cries, dwindled to a far off writhing at her feet. Her eyes passed the tall figures of mistresses in the hall, her gaze travelling to its utmost distant point to keep off what threatened to hold her attention like a burning glass. Do *their* brothers –? The thought broke from her. Her chest and throat straining, she looked round at the carefree children who seemed to mock her feelings and words came to her in the thinnest inner scream. They do, but they don't mind! In panic she searched, and found each face grotesque, directing long, volleying cries against her as her eyes fled.

When the time came she chose the longest and quietest way home, lifting her head only to be reminded by the grey streets of the years of leaden greyness to be endured.

As her eyes fixed dully upon the advertisement, bright in the sun, it seemed suddenly to heave into position, its great masses rising to show the head of a bull. She took a quick look at the old circumference, the eye, the ear and the horn set in a curling white mane, and saw that it was a complicated bull's head, liable to be misunderstood. She knew she had shaken off an intolerable burden, had reached the heavens which were always above.

Her own door stood open, making her want to rush through or be sucked in. Light gleamed everywhere from polish in the rooms, dark after sun. She found her mother talking, hand on breast, to the woman next door, the wall between them. With a need to weave herself into this pattern of peace Rose moved reverently, her head low, and began to lay the table, fearful as she passed near her mother, waiting for her reception.

Mrs Donald turned to give a calm, half-seeing look at Rose who, thus accepted, held her head upright, the better to bear the rush of gratitude. 'Here they come!' said Mrs Donald as Lennie appeared. 'No sooner one than another – who'd be a mother! It makes me think often of my poor mother and what she must have gone through!' Her mother's ghost appeared like her own creation in her head, something she could mar or make, the expression in its great eye fixed on her – its living replica – which stood, wracked. 'But we don't know half that goes on!' she cried, and saw in close-up her mother's eye, fixed and pleading for release in her, on whom her sins descended – pleading for her to absolve them by removing them from herself, as if forgiveness lay in leaving no trace. She felt the sudden impact of inherent evil, from which, striving, she must render good.

She felt the influence of Mr Matthews like a blessing in the room and paused, inspired, beneath it, drawn out of herself towards it; such sweetness came from without her, not from within.

'Aye! Here it is!' she said suddenly, her arm dramatically raised towards the boy who had knocked. 'She's gone!' she said, watching the blinds fall at the house opposite.

Mrs Donald felt steadied at the news. She felt death had come, bringing greatness to life. Looking upward, awe-stricken, she went to her bedroom. A great lurid light sprang from her eye at the sight of the white starched coat she brought out and put on. Splendid, she went to the kitchen.

'Aye! Look after things,' she said gravely to Lennie. 'Your

dinners are all in the oven. Billy's is the bottom one.' For a moment she felt that chaos would stir in her absence – that a mad dance would begin, and looking, caught Rose's craven eye helplessly craving her departure; now turned from her, watching, oblique as a bird's eye, dull with a terror that she saw must be always behind them.

'Mind!' she cried gravely, raising her arm, her eyes leaping half-heartedly to threaten. 'I'll be back in two minutes!' Then she went, banished by the child's longing for her to be gone.

# Chapter 20

The next afternoon Mrs Donald, her arms full of laundry, left the house. She bounded up to Ben as he arrived home, her face golden with smiles, melting and coy as a young girl's – as if they could meet upon only one ground – that of man and woman. She entered his house, all avidness, as she moved behind him with a sudden flash of joy and a naive, skipping step. She felt herself moving wholeheartedly, irresistibly into bliss as she saw his eye accepting her, and her arms opened to the rhythm of release. Afraid that her joy might overwhelm him, her voracious appetite for him might seem obliterating, insatiable, she felt herself to be a nightmare monster and her eyes were lurid as she held herself in.

Rose imagined his mild and drooping moustache, and the sort of twilit life with his sick wife that was all she knew of him. Now he was transfixed by her mother's great artless smiles, where emotion followed emotion, as if her wavering face were seen in water. He must not suffer, came a fierce cry from her heart – and looking up she saw that she and the rest of them belonged beneath this dark roof and were inured, but innocent, confident, she felt it couldn't happen. Lennie turned on the radio, which promptly gave a talk. Rose turned it over to dance music. He turned it back again and Rose repeated her action with never and nevermore a thought for him, and with her arms up swirled round – her own mistress.

When her mother returned Rose began to make tea, edging her way through the crowded room where Billy stood preparing for the magic evening which to Mrs Donald, as she thought of Violet, seemed like a prelude of muffled drums. She felt the horror of Violet's leaving, and the horror of this house, where each lived unaware of the others. She knew that she herself was cut off from her children, who did not see her eyes bolting with terror. She saw in Freddie's eye that he too waited for his turn to go, moving at the slightest danger, feeling himself grotesque if she caught him unemployed. With wonderful defiance, exulting in the debacle, she sat clutching the chair. Let them go! she triumphed, and felt the impact of her strength flood back and thought, Oh, how she would make them pay! But she knew, constricted, it was herself who must break, and a blessing came as she accepted this with conscious suffering.

'A clean shirt, Ma?' asked Billy.

'You've had a good wash I suppose?' she replied, seeing vividly how dirty he was. 'A bucket of water over you, that's what you want my lad, like my father up at six every morning then up and out, and a day's work done before breakfast!'

'I thought he was up at seven?' said Billy, amused.

'Aye! Never you mind! Think yourself lucky he's not here to this day. If he were there'd be a difference – and in more ways than one. Then you'd laugh on the other side of your face m'lad and show more respect to your mother!'

'Good job he's not here then!' he muttered.

'Aye!' She turned on him, 'Is that the way to talk of the dead? I suppose you'll say the same of your mother when she's dead and gone! I'm not long for this world! The way I feel I could go any day and I shan't be sorry –!' And looking up she suddenly saw the absurdity of her ideas about Ben, the unreality of pleasure and the nearness of doom.

'Why, what's the matter with you?' he asked playfully.

'Aye! It would take more than you and your sort to know

what's wrong with me. Broken-hearted!' She cried out the epic word, her sinful self a sudden mountain upon her. 'And having to cater for a lot of tykes into the bargain who'd no more give a thought to their mother – a widowed woman – than Tom, Dick or Harry!'

Billy sat down to his tea, and Mrs Donald was glad to serve him. She called in Rose and Freddie and they sat, either side of the fender, sharing a cup. It seemed to Rose that she was being her real self in this room, that things were really always like this and everything else was a mistake and a dream. Mrs Donald, pleased to see her unafraid, felt an atmosphere of comfort in the room. She felt her mind expand and her sight extend. In accepting them she felt a new balance in which she was, herself, diminished. She saw faces she knew lit up for the first time, faces from which, like her own, she had been cut off – as though those beneath her who she had thought she had ruled were now seen as equals to be enjoyed for the first time.

Rose suddenly shouted, her joy bubbling up, and the spirit she showed in ignoring her mother made Mrs Donald feel that her every blow was a boomerang – useless except to crush herself.

'Aye!' she screamed with a vibrating pointing finger, softened to genuine anger by the arrested children. 'Any more and you'll be upstairs. It's always the same!' she cried to Billy. 'Give them an inch and they take a yard!'

'How's religion, Rose?' asked Billy, who noticed her with sudden novelty, 'Still following the Lord?' He rose smiling. 'Can you see him and speak to him? Does he answer your prayers?'

'Yes!' she answered weakly, and lifting her head, Rose saw that the supreme test was upon her and that she would fail. 'Yes, yes!' she cried, and seeing she lied he brayed, delighted by the rare diversion.

'But it doesn't stop her thieving and lying – the thief!' began Mrs Donald, who saw in Rose a world beyond her reach. 'Look at the sausages on Saturday, and can I turn and leave my purse for a minute? You can't trust her out of your sight!'

Rose, back at her station by the sink, cried out at the injustice. 'I didn't touch those sausages, and you've been on at me all the week!' Mrs Donald leapt up and was almost upon her when Rose, despairing, lifted her head, unafraid. She met the child's fearless eye and turned back. Lifting dishes and washing them Rose looked within herself, exulting, triumphant. She had a weapon of such marvellous power she hardly knew what it was! She went over what had happened. She had looked at her mother fearlessly as she came on. Rose staggered as one might who looked at a tiger, and seeing her once more fall back, Rose exulted. She saw herself wielding, perfecting a weapon; then saw with emptiness what this triumph must cost – that she stood above with her mother beneath her – and, though still exulting, loathed it.

'I'm going now, Ma!' said Billy.

'Aye! I'll have your money before you do,' she said.

'Gave it to you last night, didn't I?' he murmured, sounding her distracted memory.

'Aye! None of that this week, m'lad – I'm not such a fool as you'd like to think. If you gave it to me where is it? I haven't a penny for the milkman and he'll be here in a minute.'

'You've probably hidden it,' he said, amused. 'We'll have a marvellous time when you've gone, Ma – pound notes stuffed everywhere.' He laughed while she joined with him in the irresistible treasure-hunt.

There was a knock on the door and, turning towards it, Mrs Donald's head swivelled back to the scullery where the shock had abruptly ended a silent scuffle.

'It's the milkman, Ma.' Mrs Donald started towards the front door, her rage boiling as she wondered what they had been up to – the twisters.

Calming herself she saw the terrible power in herself and gloated that she must still dominate and rule. With a pound note in her hand she went out to the milkman, looking up at the house across the road where her hopes had become all dreams – where the amalgamation of homes, his with hers, was now baulked by a shadow in which she saw Ben, anchored, sombre and immovable. She recognized her tragic blindness, and with a thrill of alarm became aware of his secret burrowing, while she openly flashed light. She saw the hugeness of her lust in his shrinking look – determined to get away, forever holding her at arms length while he fled; and as she dropped her eyes for cover she felt the lurid, guarded flash of an escaping secret. The milkman counted change into her hand.

'You didn't give me the pound,' he said, looking at her politely.

'Well, where is it?' she gasped. 'It can't have walked, it was in my hand when I came to this door – it can't have disappeared. Look again!' she cried out, moving away. 'If you're not twisted by one you're twisted by the other!'

'You didn't give it me!' he cried threateningly, and as she closed the door upon him he hurled insults at her which she heard her neighbours hear.

Rose, too, heard the row and felt as if some shameful birthmark were exposed to the whole street. Her mother returned, bounding into the kitchen – reared up threateningly like some great bird.

'You're a beautiful son!' she cried at Billy as she raced to the scullery. 'Standing there while your mother's being insulted – and what was going on there?' she muttered avidly, her eyes narrowing upon Rose and Freddie, whose eyes widened. 'Look at them! Sly as they make 'em!' she cried as they stood, aghast, backs to the wall as she bounded towards them. She felt her hands aching to lay hold, to sink her rage into his shrinking flesh – she saw herself as the age-old monster licking blood. 'It's not as if I don't try with them,' she cried into the teeth of it. 'You saw what happened this very afternoon, and what she's like outside the house God only knows!' This thought filled her with such rage that she leapt with sudden uncontrollable ferocity upon Rose, hammering her head with the knife she held, pulling and clawing at the skin and flesh until her breath came short and she longed to stop. But she was possessed, caught up until the death, until the other broke. Tears came dropping in a great involuntary consummation which she felt blindly in an awful spasm on her face. But Rose, buried in her mother's great bulk, fought back. Swerving to avoid a blow she caught hold of a great breast, horrified as her fingers sank into the soft flesh.

'Did you see that! Did you see how she pulled me?' muttered Mrs Donald with deadly intent. 'Give it to her, Billy!'

Billy let swing his heavy numb hand, loosely strung and swinging from the shoulder in a terrible blow that brought blood to Rose's mouth.

Rose gave out a demented shriek and tore herself free. Overwhelmed by humiliation, lost in its unutterable depths where words couldn't reach, her cries became that of a child in paroxysm. 'I'm going,' she shrieked, bolting for the door as words came, relieving her in a great, final denial: 'I'm going, I'm going, and never coming back!'

Running now as emotion rose, possessed by an errand she

could not resist, she rapped on the door of the widower, Ben. Before his humble figure she danced like flame, ever moving away as if she warned him of fire, and her words were uttered with terrible necessity. 'Don't marry my mother. You will hate it. It is terrible in our house – we have a terrible life – and with you it will be just the same!'

# Chapter 21

When she heard Rose creep in Mrs Donald felt her life return. She heard the girl climbing the stairs, dragging her misery up. She longed to go to her but held herself back, incapable of any good, raising her head manically to accept her guilt. She saw the roof above her dark with terror like a death that she'd created. She was given time to see the terrible nadir from which she fled, denying it.

She saw herself in the eye of Mr Matthews as if in a light from outside, a monster which knew its days were numbered, and the fact that she had seen came as balm to her reason, as if the very viewpoint had put it away, meant she had left it behind. Mr Matthews knew her – the very fact meant hope, was a coherent eye in which her thoughts were shared and given back with a sharpness that seemed to warn of greater evil to come. She longed, in terror, to take her life back, felt the crushing weight of its ill effects, that in the future she could no more act but only mourn what she had done.

She felt in Rose an earnest of Violet's return. Not to her bosom, that forfeit state of bliss, but to heal the breach constricting the girl's breath. She knew if they met now her hatred would show – as if she looked into the eye of great revulsion, the taunting girl would reflect her hatred back from the image of her she hated. She knew she had stumbled upon something that must bring her very low, as if from this spot to which she clung the evil involving them began and ended. She must wait quietly until she saw Violet, prepare for this in everything she did, set right those wrongs which had them by the throat. She clapped her hands to her face to bear the goodness of it, her only joy in the past. She saw herself greeting Violet. The smile stretching her face as if breaking new ground was the smile that she had seen on the face of Mr Matthews, who had long ago seen and inaugurated this, and had taken upon himself half the burden. She felt at that moment that they were in touch – as if she had conjoined with her true self in a beatitude in which she must become like that saint from whom she was divided as from her true self. She could go, if she must, to the school but she knew that their business was not in each other but in sharing the same vision, and that the love which took her hideousness from her, which she felt rising, lifted from her, was the greatest, by far, that she could reach. She saw her life before her in a transformation she had known all along, whispered in words that once heard could never return to the void.

She went into the yard trilling a hymn, slashing greenery for cuttings and plunging them into the earth with a wonderful sensation of the joy of life. Yet she still felt the great, gloating eye of chaos inside her, denying all this – an eye which she must always watch with the eye of her own vision, to which she held on in her mind as she went towards it.

# Epilogue

My mother was born Mary Lilian Hunt in May 1921 at 62 Clemence St, Limehouse, the fifth child of Maud and Edward Hunt. While the children were still small their father was electrocuted at work. Although he lived he became permanently deranged and was committed to a mental hospital. From time to time his wife would bring him home, and it was during one of these visits that he got the children out of bed, brought them downstairs and blessed them, as Mrs Donald recalls in the book. He died just before Mary was born.

My grandmother was left with five young children and no support, and for a time the children were put into an orphanage which my mother remembered as a haven. Every morning she would climb up to an airing cupboard to get a clean sheet for a little boy who wet his bed. When she left the orphanage he wept so bitterly that she told him she would be coming back soon; she always thought of this lie as one of the bad things she had done in her life.

In the late twenties Mrs Hunt was married again to William Bain MacDonald, a marine engineer who my mother recalled only as a 'just man'. He also was killed in an industrial accident while working in the hold of a ship.

Most of my grandmother's life was spent in grinding poverty, and Mary reacted with despair to the unrelieved grey and dirt of her surroundings. She used to long for a school uniform and her only escape from the misery was to go on occasional camping trips with the Guides.

When she was about eleven years old her mother sent her out to buy paraffin. She dropped the money she had been given and could not retrieve the final ha'penny from the rush matting that covered the floor. Rather than confess to her mother she crossed the main road to a shop where paraffin was cheaper. No doubt half oblivious, as so often Rose is in the book, she was knocked down by a lorry, and lost her right foot as a result. She was unconscious in hospital for a fortnight after the accident. When recovering at home she was left immured in a bedroom with a young baby. She would pinch the child to make it cry and so bring someone up from downstairs. Finally she had an hysterical fit which so impressed her mother that she brought her down. She was taken away from the local school where she had been doing well and sent to a 'cripple school' where the headmistress was a dipsomaniac, and so her education came to an end.

She ignored her disability and very few people who knew her were aware of it. She refused to wear all the tackle that was supposed to keep her false limb attached, and kept it on seemingly by sheer willpower. Augustus John insulted her once, and ended by saying she only had one leg. She replied, 'You're wrong there, I've got three!'

From the time she was fourteen or fifteen, she made constant attempts to run away from home. She could only get work in the sewing sweatshops in and around Commercial Road, and the money was not sufficient to pay both for a room, and for her keep. She would therefore starve, and cringe in trams, hoping to pass unnoticed, afraid of being asked for the fare. She remembered a Christmas with no food, until her landlady brought up a plate; and the woman's pity was the worst of all.

Then one day in the street she met an anthropologist

called Kilton Stewart. No doubt impressed by her great beauty, he asked her to stay at his flat. She said, 'No funny business,' and went with him. She was at this time about sixteen, and completely innocent. Kilton Stewart had several people staying at his flat, frequenters of Soho and Fitzrovia. He was concerned for her health, and later sent her to friends in the country, who fed her well, and persuaded her to take baths. Cedric Morris's first art school, 'The Pound' at Dedham, was nearby, and she modelled there. Lucien Freud was then studying at the school.

It is not easy to account in detail for the time until she married Ralph Keene in January 1941. She rented different rooms at different times in many parts of London. Some she left without going back to get her things. She found she was entitled to a small disability pension, previously paid to her mother, and this enabled her just to survive. She remembered how she used to walk down Oxford Street in the small hours to eat porridge at Lyons Corner House on the way home, and how she thought of it as luxury if she could afford cream with the porridge. This was the only food she could later recall eating at this period.

Tambimuttu has recorded that she lived for a time in Fitzrovia. He met her at the Coffee An' café, where one evening she sang, and stripped off her blouse and bra. Elements of the scene in the book where Violet makes her triumphal visit to the Soho café would come from this time. She went a great deal to Soho, and to the Café Royal. She visited her mother occasionally. Mrs MacDonald was bombed out twice during the war, and moved to Wanstead.

She fell in love with Louis MacNeice, so much so that she found she could not utter a word in his presence. Nothing came of this passion, although he wrote a passage about her in his poem 'The Kingdom':

Too large in feature for a world of cuties,
Too sculptured for a cocktail lounge flirtation,
This girl is almost awkward, carrying off
The lintel of convention on her shoulders,
A Doric river-goddess with a pitcher
Of ice-cold wild emotions. Pour them where she will
The pitcher will not empty nor the stream grow warm
But is so cold it burns . . .

Mary Keene was not a bohemian. She said she lost her
East End accent overnight when she realised how ugly the
sounds were; her new accent had slight upper-class inton-
ations. She was always looking for a grander and freer world
than the one she knew. She was interested in politics, and
later – in her fifties – she joined the Labour Party.

Tambimuttu has said he was the one who introduced
Mary to Ralph Keene. She said they met in a night club
during a wartime police raid. Ralph Keene admired her tan
and extricated her safely from the melée. She was nineteen,
he was forty, and he had had a varied career. He owned a
fleet of fishing boats at one time; then he worked at Tooth's as
an art dealer. Later he became a film director and producer,
with considerable success. Mary Keene loved his elegance
and ease, saying that she only realised later that she married
him because she had become so exhausted with fending for
herself.

Ralph Keene had been Matthew Smith's dealer at
Tooth's, and introduced him to his new wife later in 1941.
They met constantly after this, and Smith painted a large
number of canvases of her during the 1940s. He attempted to
teach Mary how to ride a bicycle, and Ralph Keene was
angry with her for her lack of consideration in allowing 'an
old man' to run beside her. She did not think of him as old,

however, although he was then just over sixty.

The Keenes moved to a pretty house, 1 Selwood Place on the borders of Chelsea a year or two after their marriage. One day when Mary was walking Matthew Smith to the bus stop from there, they saw an advertisement for a furnished flat at the Chelsea Cloisters, which Smith took, remaining there until his death in 1959. A neighbour at Selwood Place was Poppet, the elder daughter of Augustus John, and it may have been at about this time that she introduced Mary Keene to Dig Yorke, who then introduced her to her husband, the writer Henry Green. With the Yorkes and others Mary Keene went to the Gargoyle, the Cavendish, the Ritz and other fashionable haunts.

Taste and style were very important to her. In both she tended to be restrained. At the same time she loved glamour, and clothes, and had one or two beautiful dresses made. She was slim and blonde, with burning white skin; a friend recalled that people fell silent when she walked into a room.

Mary Keene introduced Smith to the Yorkes and they became close friends. Matthew Smith painted two large canvases of Henry Green. It was said when Green's novel *Concluding* was published in 1948 that the character of Rock was based on Smith, but Mary Keene never heard this confirmed. She thought that Elizabeth, Rock's granddaughter, was partly drawn from herself.

I was born in May 1944, and a number of changes followed. Mary Keene broke with her mother, and did not see her again before her death in 1949. She also arrived at a final leavetaking with Ralph Keene, and they were later divorced. Mary went to stay with the Thomases, at Newquay; she was a friend of Caitlin Thomas for years, also of old Mrs Thomas, Dylan's mother. She did not hold a very high opinion of Dylan Thomas, rather scorning his comics and bags of sweets. After they moved to Laugharne she bought a little cottage there, where we went for school holidays.

She went on to stay at Fordingbridge for about three months towards the end of 1944. She sat to Augustus John every day, and a number of good drawings resulted. Matthew Smith was also invited to Fordingbridge at her suggestion, and the two masters painted their portraits of each other at this time.

Eventually Matthew Smith helped her to set up in a flat, 15 Cheyne Place, in Chelsea. About 1949 we left there and went to 9 Drayton Court, near the Fulham Road. I believe Smith paid the rent. Apart from this we lived on a tiny allowance from Ralph Keene, and were always worried about money.

We stayed at Drayton Court until 1961. It was an ugly flat, and my memories of our life there are gloomy. It may be that my mother liked it originally because it was modern; she was always interested in modern things, and in the future. Nostalgia was anathema to her.

In 1950 she had a child by Matthew Smith. He did not want her to go through with the pregnancy, and they parted for a time; this caused them both so much pain that they never quarrelled again. The baby died in the first days after her birth.

For years after this, it seems to me now, my mother saw virtually no one but Matthew Smith and myself, apart from the people we met on the holidays in Wales. The relationship between Matthew Smith and Mary Keene was happy only in moments. It was difficult for her to define. She was not his mistress, nor his daughter, nor his grandaughter. They loved each other, and were mutually dependent, and yet independence was very important to both of them. My own relationship with my mother was not easy. There was some violence in it, but never on the scale that appears in the book. She was very loving by nature, and highly responsive to other people. It followed that she devoted the greater part of her energies to me for many years. I came before her writing, which meant, nevertheless, a very great deal to her. As a child this seemed quite obvious to me, and the only possible order of things. However I always felt that she threw me, in a way, off-balance. Her eyes were extraordinary: enormous, piercing and very expressive. I often felt I retreated before them, and this upset her and called forth her scorn. She believed pride was her besetting sin, and yet it had, of course, an intimate connection with her magnificent spirit and courage.

In the fifties we began going to church. Initially Mary Keene's religion was formal and Anglo-Catholic. She had a great admiration for T.S. Eliot's writing and ideas, and we walked quite some way each Sunday to the Church that he attended. It is in this period that the genesis of *Mrs Donald* lies. Later her religious ideas changed considerably, and she became devoted to the writings of Simone Weil. She always read a very great deal, very widely, and was often carried away with enthusiasm.

When Matthew Smith died in 1959 he made Mary Keene his heir. She herself died in 1981 at the age of sixty.

The process of writing *Mrs Donald* was long-drawn-out. Pages of small, densely packed writing were distilled into the short scenes which appear in the book. Some years after she started to write Mary conceived the idea that Rose, Violet and Mrs Donald should be the same person at different stages of life. She was very excited by this idea, which was suggested to some extent perhaps by certain passages of T.S. Eliot's *Four Quartets*. She wrote out shortly before she died, when she read through *Mrs Donald* for the last time:

We must be still and still moving
Unto another intensity
For a further union, a deeper communion. ('East Coker')

It is suggested in the book that Mrs Donald was herself
ill-treated as a child. Mary Keene thought that as a young
woman her mother had loved a tugboat captain, but ended
by marrying the wrong man, just as Violet does. Mary
thought that this wrong action destroyed her mother's
natural lines of communication, which were very necessary
to someone with such a large and unruly temperament. She
was thus predisposed to madness. Similarly, in the closing
pages of the book Violet also is unable to talk openly of her
pregnancy, because of its illicit origin.

The mainspring of the book is of course Mary Keene's
painful involvement in the predicament of the battered child
and the persecuting parent, a vicious circle if ever there was
one. She was not satisfied merely to record scenes and sensations. For her it was necessary to attempt to redeem the
past by bringing her character, Mrs Donald, to a point where
she can begin to realise the possibility of escape from her
intolerable conditions.

When the book begins Mrs Donald, as a mad person, is
conscious only of herself, outside reality which even when she
can see it simply baffles her. Some movement starts when she
is amazed at the swiftness with which extreme and opposite
emotions can arise and subside within her. Then comes her
contact with Mr Matthews, who as a result of his Christian
belief takes upon himself the weight of a genuine meeting
with her. She divines his intentions, and through this she can
begin to see her daughters as a separate entity. This is the
beginning of the end of madness, and the start of a long
struggle towards the realisation of her true self.

The redemption of the past so desired by Mary Keene is attained, I believe, in the writing and, finally, in the publication of this book.

ALICE KEENE, 1983